PAINT

by Ayah

first published by Ayah in 2018
Copyright © Ayah, 2018

ISBN: 978-1-7327773-0-9

Library of Congress Control Number: 2018912163

Any references to historical events, real people, or real places are used fictitiously. Names, characters, and places are products of the author's imagination.

This book is the first in a trilogy.

First Print Edition 2018.

"God has heard the words of the woman who disputed with you about her husband and complained to God: God has heard what you both had to say."
—Qur'an, 58:1

"I am only resolved to act in that manner which will, in my own opinion, constitute my happiness, without reference to *you,* or to any person so wholly unconnected with me."
—Elizabeth Bennet (from the novel *Pride and Prejudice*)

PAINT

I

ANIMAL

Standing outside my favorite bakery for the first time in months, I wondered if people in town thought I killed my husband.

I wondered if they were right.

Lifting my hat, I swiped a hand across my forehead. Despite myself, I heard the inner mantra of my subconscious, the words that haunted me since the day that Andreas died: *Men are strange. Ruled by their organs. I don't understand it. It was an accident.*

I'd come to appreciate hats a great deal more after Andreas's passing. They have a way of determining affect that leave people content to judge you without asking questions. Perfect for a young widow in mourning. Of course, I realize all this now, but I wouldn't have thought it when I was twenty-eight. I'm having all manner of insights since I decided to share the story of my adventure with Antony.

If you're reading this, watching my voice and my being from the depths of your imaginative vision, I ask only one thing from you: don't be afraid to use color.

I peered into the shop window and didn't recognize the boy behind the pastry counter. He must have been new. I was tempted to go back home, but I'd spent too much time there of late. Turning around, I saw yet another new feature on the block: an enormous painting leaning on a condemned building.

It was an animal without eyes, yet it conveyed a sentience that excited me. The painting I noticed first, its maker second. To this day I don't know how that could have happened. There is little more noticeable than Antony.

At the time, he was tucked in a large brown coat, sitting next to the painting with one foot poised in front of it, at once relaxed and defensive. When a pedestrian happened to pause before the painting, the boy looked at it, too, trying (and failing) to hide a smile. When I saw this, I went into the bakery.

"I have a question," I demanded of the stranger behind the counter.

"Are you getting anything?"

I blinked. "Um. Well, yes, I want a chocolate crown. Do you know that painter across the street?"

"We don't make chocolate crowns anymore."

I tore my gaze from the window and gave him a pleading look. "Why?"

"I'm not sure, ma'am. But we have these fresh doughnuts, you can get any flavor cream to fill it."

"Very well." I waved my hand. "Two of those, please. Do you know the young man across the street?"

The boy snapped open a sheet of wax paper. "Only a little. Decent fellow, from what I hear."

Five minutes later I crossed the street with an armful of warm doughnuts, growing wary of the painter. He was a man I didn't know. I steeled myself and handed him one of the pastries. "Young man? This is for you."

He stared at me. "Are you sure?" The slight pucker of curiosity in his face was dangerously disarming. I relaxed a little, feeling like I'd met him in another life.

"I'm sure. It's a gift."

"Thank you, ma'am." I was standing so far away he had to reach the extent of his arm forward to take it. A glob of cream swelled out of the doughnut.

I looked uncertainly behind me, then back at the painting. "What's your name?"

"I'm Antony." He licked the cream. "Without an H."

"Are you selling this painting?"

Antony's voice declined with resignation. "Yes, ma'am. For five grand. But of course," he waved an arm. "You can look at it for free."

I dug through my handbag. "Do you have a way to transport it?"

"No, ma'am. In fact, I—what are you doing?"

"I'm buying your painting."

Antony stood. "Stop it."

"I'm in the city. I can give you this check, or I can buy a lot of other things I don't need."

He looked at the painting, then back at me. I feared he might be unwilling to part with it. Then he said: "I'm not a derelict."

"What's your full name?"

"I'm not a derelict. I work, you know. I paint houses. And storefronts. I do signage."

I looked up at him; he was taller than I expected. "My name is Eva Hayworth, and I love your painting. What is so wrong with that?"

"Nothing, Miss Hayworth, I'm sorry." He looked cowed.

"Good." I smiled, turning back to my check. Can you tell me the rest of your name, now?"

He shook his head. "I don't know it." A pause happened. "I'm sorry if my work misled you. My name is not reputable among patrons such as yourself."

I dropped my arms. "You can't be serious, boy. My tastes are hardly a slave to the whims of society, thank you very much." I laughed a little. "I'm hardly in a position to care about reputation."

Antony wore a blank, unassuming expression. When it didn't change, I felt a funny lightness. He had never even heard of me. I told him I had a driver waiting and offered to pay him by cash at my estate.

"Perhaps you could help me mount the painting?" I asked.

Antony looked over my shoulder. "Who else is with you?"

"No one," I said, and then made an internal note that that was unwise of me to say this, even if he was being more cautious than I. I sighed. Perhaps he had heard of me, after all.

Antony crossed his arms. "All right, bring the car around."

My driver, Edgar Pike, had straw-colored hair. He looked old and young at the same time, but not in a sophisticated way. When he smiled, his eyes did not. My late husband trusted him implicitly, and this was one of a few points of contention between us. But over the years, Pike had proved reliable. At least insofar as his driving duties were concerned. I had no reason to replace him.

I remember that Pike stared at Antony far too long for my liking, but he helped load the painting into the back. It's maker jolted at every bump in the road, as if his body could brace itself on behalf of the canvas. It was a romantic notion, I thought, but then, maybe he just wasn't used to being in a car.

"Antony?"

"Yes, Miss Hayworth?"

"What is the painting called?"

"Painting," he answered.

"Yes, the painting," I clarified.

He continued: *"Painting* is the name."

I nodded. "Painting as in the action or painting as in the thing itself?"

"Both."

"Oh." My voice softened. "I think gerunds are very misunderstood." We started to smile at each other and then hit a crack in the road.

It's a long drive back from the city. Antony was wiping sweat off his face with the front of his shirt, blushing as he did so. He seemed eager to escape my observation. He hid his face by turns with the window and his hands. The hands were veined in a pattern different from most that of most men. A tendon twitched under the skin of his forearm. He removed his coat.

"Are you okay?"

"I'm all right, Miss Hayworth. I'm not well suited to motion.."

"We're nearly there."

Upon arrival, he wanted to carry the painting himself and declined help from my butler (whose name, as I duly noted in the man's interview, was actually Butler). I trailed behind Antony with the brown coat. Butler offered to help me, and I also rejected in an effort to give the boy's behavior some precedent.

We went upstairs and paused outside my bedroom doorway.

"I want it hung across from my bed."

"Your *bed*, Miss Hayworth?" Antony asked from behind the canvas. I understood his confusing. The painting was a mess of hot color and it wouldn't suit most bedrooms.

"Yes, I want it in the bedroom. Go on in, it's…it's to your left."

The painting seemed to float in the room of its own accord. Then it rotated, revealing Antony on the other side. He set it against the wall. "Where does the morning light come in?"

"Over there." I pointed at the dresser. "It makes the jewelry blink." Up until then, Antony's tone had only been curious or appeasing. He sounded confident, now.

"Where does it set?"

I pointed again. Antony stood at the end of my bed and scanned the wall. "It's not a bad spot. I'll need some hardware." He looked at me. "To hang it."

"Oh, right. I'll go and inquire."

Later, I sat on my bed and watched. Antony had his back to me, his arms stretched to meet the edges of the painting. It dramatically expanded his effect. My payment was in his back pocket, and I realized I couldn't remember the last time a man was in my bedroom. Except when they took Andy's body away.

"How old are you, Antony?"

"I'm nearly twenty—" He dropped a nail, then kneeled laboriously to pick it up. "Nearly twenty-seven."

"And you're painting houses, are you? Have you got anything else to do?" Brown-coated rascal.

"I really like the paint, I guess." He stepped backwards and tilted his head. "It's not straight."

It was perfectly straight. I couldn't believe him. "It looks fine."

"I'll fix it," he said simply.

"Okay." Guilt curled in my gut. It felt predatory to be watching him, but I couldn't help myself. He was starting to sweat. He smelled different than Andreas. It made me feel sleepy. "Do you wear a paint mask to keep you from delirium?" I asked.

He made a noncommittal noise. To this day I rarely see a man willing to hold a conversation while he's immersed in another activity.

"I've seen them," I went on, "with the lobes on the sides. There are fumes in the paint, you now. They float up and smack you in the face."

Antony breathed in a gust. "Is that to your satisfaction?"

"Yes, that's perfect." I grinned. "Would you stay for tea?"

"No thank you, ma'am. It's a long way back to town."

"Indeed. I'd see you out, but I want to be here the moment this becomes mine." I nodded at the painting.

"I understand." He tilted his head. "Thank you, Miss Hayworth. Please take good care of *Painting.*"

"I will. You can give your address to Pike. He'll take you back to town." When he left the room I sat still, ruminating. After moments, like the echo of a hope bell his voice flickered back through the doorway.

"Miss Hayworth?"

"Yes?"

"I don't have an address." A pause happened. "What can I tell your driver?"

I stared at the doorway for a moment. No address at all? I believed it, but surely he knew of some place in the city where he could be dropped off?

"Well," I said, trying to keep my face impassive, "he's not one to solve such hiccups on his own. I'll go and talk to him."

"Where can I wait?"

On the bed, I thought, suppressing a sudden chill.

I pointed outside the room. "Just there, and don't you wander my house."

I went downstairs, glancing back once. He stood waiting for me. I turned into the nearest hallway and fell back against the wall once I was sure I had left his field of vision. No address! With a talent like that? How terribly vulnerable he must be. And so young. I shook my head. Barely a year without a husband and I was already losing my senses about the first new chap to come along.

My search for Pike was slow and colored by these thoughts. I was curious, though, about whether Antony had even made a real attempt to leave. When I found Pike in the front room, I asked him about it.

"The boy doesn't know his address," he said, barely looking at me. "I told him he ought to get that sorted out before I make such a long drive back. Call his work, at least. I'm a driver, not a navigator."

Obnoxious, was what he was. "Don't let me see you being unkind to him, Pike."

"Certainly, Madame, I can bear with it—,"

"I hope so," I said, and walked away from him. I was near an idea; I chased it down the hall and into the drawing room, scowling at the wallpaper in there. Viciously ugly. Andreas had it imported as a gift. His intentions were so pure that I couldn't bring myself to complain. And like Pike, it wasn't worth the effort to replace. Not in a world where personal drivers (and wallpaper) were dwindling fast.

Antony stood waiting with his hands behind his back. I felt curiosity emanating from his posture. I invited him downstairs and into the drawing room.

He made a face. "Ugh."

"It's hideous, Antony. Am I right? I mean, look at it."

"Mm. Awful. Have you considered a window?"

"Well, I have, but it doesn't connect to the outside. And anyway, my husband…" I suddenly became aware of some hair in my face. I pushed it behind my ear. "My late husband thought it was special because it was printed in Europe or some faraway thing like that. I told him I love orchids."

Antony frowned. "But those aren't orchids."

"I know," I said with pity. "He thought they were."

He hadn't thought they were. But how could I know? Wasn't it good form to assume the best of the dead?

"He was generous to me," I said, and it wasn't untrue. "But you know what I've been thinking? I've been thinking a painting of a window would be nice."

"A painting of a window…"

"Yes."

"Or a painting that's a window?"

I puzzled over this. I might have found Antony's focus on semantics to be irksome, if he had the habit of over explaining himself as men tend to do. But he kept quiet and patiently awaited my response. "A painting that's a window," I decided aloud. "Do you work on commission?"

"That depends, Miss Hayworth."

"Depends on what?"

He shrugged and smiled.

I returned it. "Would you fancy a walk? I'd like to show you something."

Antony's coat had enormous lapels that flapped obscenely in the breeze. I led him to a second house on my estate, a small apartment of sorts, with a studio attached to it. It used to be Andy's. It had gathered dust since his demise. I was glad not to be reentering it alone.

Antony had a wonderful interaction with the studio's interior. He touched nothing until he saw the kitchen sink and leaned in to examine the spout. Then he suddenly went still and I realized he'd become aware of my gaze.

"This was supposed to be my husband's workspace," I said, "but I don't think he really made anything."

"You're right," Antony said softly. "The floor is too clean. I love the windows in here." He looked at me. "Did you want to restore the garden outside?"

"Not especially. Maybe. Why?"

"I could restore it for you. I can do a lot of things, if you have any more jobs for me."

"I do. I want you to stay here and make a painting for the drawing room."

"Here?"

"Yes."

He reached for a nearby stool and sat on it. "Thank you," he said in silence that followed. "I'd love to, Miss Hayworth, I really want that, but it's an ambitious endeavor. I mean, it's very costly."

"It is a commission," I emphasized. "You can buy whatever you need."

"I'm not a notable, ma'am," he continued, "I don't deserve this kind of investment."

I crossed my arms. "This isn't about you or your reputation. I just want a damn good painting." I felt a rioting heat every time he expressed this self-abasing attitude, and I couldn't tell whether it was from disgust or pleasure. "I want something to neutralize that caustic wallpaper, and I'm convinced that you can do it with the proper resources. Are you willing or not?"

By octave his voice sensuously dropped: "I'm always willing, Miss Hayworth."

"Good. Then I will direct Pike to take you back to the city for supplies. Take your time and don't let him pester you, understand?"

He was grinning. "Yes, ma'am."

I watched Antony get in the car. I'd given him a blank check and wondered why I wasn't nervous. It was a real test of faith. Or foolishness. But then, I did keep most of my money in a personal safe.

This is it, Eva, I thought to myself as I went up to my room. *Enjoy the last night of your fortune before the boy robs you blind.* I stared at my new painting. He'd run me out of my home, I thought, perhaps take *Painting* back. Maybe he'd leave with the brown coat, for irony's sake. It probably smells like him. I'd have to wear it, though, Fall is nearing winter and the streets are harsh. I bet he'd love this house. He'd take my room and sleep in my bed, laughing to himself for fooling a widow.

In my library, I perused half-read books and read a hundred pages between them. The thought of Antony's commission distracted me as much as the memory of his shoulders, so I went back up to my room to look longer at what I had of him. He'd take my fortune, alright. My jewelry, too. Maybe he'd wear it in triumph. What a sight.

I heard knocking and stretched on the bed. "I'm coming, Butler."

"You have a phone call."

I nodded, stretching my arms. "I'll go and get it." My phone was a funny thing. Its shape reminded me of Chinese carvings of horses or drawings of silly ducks. I picked up its nose. "Hello?"

"Is this Miss Hayworth?"

"Yes, Antony."

"I hope you can hear me."

"Yes, I can hear you just—,"

"—Calling from the *bank*, Miss Hayworth, from the *bank* because you have accidentally given me a blank check!"

"Antony! Lower your voice, for heaven's sake, I can hear you. I know I gave you a blank check. You are to write in your estimated cost and then cash it."

"Miss Hayworth!" There was a pause. "Are you sure? I feel the need to tell you—can you hear me?"

"Yes."

"I was going to say you shouldn't give people blank checks or they will think you are wet behind the ears." His voice had the tinny, halting quality of someone who's never had their own phone.

"Well, Antony, it's terribly naïve of you to announce that in a bank, don't you think?"

"Miss Hayworth I'm talking into the phone now—,"

"Yes, but everyone around can still hear you. Now listen, you're the one who didn't take a look at the thing before I gave it to you. Just stuffed it in your pocket."

"Miss Hayworth?"

"Yes."

"The teller of the bank says there must be an amount—,"

"Look, Antony, I've already signed the check. You'll write in your amount and take it back to the teller, alright?"

"Yes, ma'am." Another pause. "I'm going to end the phone, now." I heard several seconds of shuffling, and when he finally hung up, I laughed. He was by turns brazen and demure. He'd likely forget to buy his own groceries.

I was too busy over the next two weeks to see him. I had meetings with a financial advisor, and a lawyer who was supposed to help me straighten out the problems of Society, but it seemed that I was straightening out more napkins and pillows than anything else. In retrospect, I can't even remember the subject of our conversations.

I spent a great deal of time writing a proposal for a literacy program, but no one seemed able to understand what I was trying to say.

Antony had a key to the house so he could scope out the drawing room at his leisure. I visited it often, hoping a little that I might run into him, but I never did. I found myself leaving personal belongings in there and memorizing their arrangements in case a change in pattern could reveal his presence, his effect on environment, his picking things up and putting them down. But my things gathered dust.

Well into this game, I asked Butler, (while I was pretending to read), whether he'd seen Antony, and he said that he hadn't.

"That worries me a touch," I said. "I gave him work to do, you know."

"Yes, my lady, I'm well aware."

"It was a nice thing to do. It was nice to give him a job, and I'm right in thinking that it should be done well. I'm surprised you haven't seen him stepping about."

"My lady?"

"Yes, Butler?"

"Why don't you go and see his progress for yourself? It is a commission, after all."

I lowered my book. I couldn't believe I hadn't thought of that. Somehow I didn't feel justified in visiting, but I couldn't see why not. "I suppose I'll go this afternoon."

"My lady?"

"Yes, Butler?"

"It is afternoon."

While walking there I delighted in the thought of keeping an active dialogue with my charge. Perhaps I could invite him for tea. I'd grown used to isolation and longed for a break in routine.

When I got there, his windows were open to the breeze. He looked at me with sleepless eyes. "Good afternoon, Miss Hayworth."

"Good afternoon. You haven't been in touch, Antony, I was wondering about the painting. I gave you a key for a reason."

"A key?"

I blinked rapidly as he invited me further into the house. "Yes. A key. I gave you a key so that you might examine the drawing room."

He grit his teeth. A look of repressed frustration passed over his face and with it, his hand. "Miss Hayworth, I must be such a grievance to you."

"What makes you say that? I haven't said that!"

He motioned me into the studio with an arm. Notebooks and paper samples lay about like the casualties of a battle. Dominating the central space was an enormous stretched canvas. It was empty. I averted my gaze. "I see you've got the canvas together."

"Stretched it myself."

"These are interesting," I pointed to one of his notebooks. It had a bright swirl not unlike the shapes in *Painting*. I looked around and saw it elsewhere. "Is this your muse or something? This swirling shape?"

"You could say that. I call her Play. It's silly, I know."

"Is this in all your paintings?"

"Usually, but…" Antony flung his head backwards and huffed. "I've had a lot of trouble with this commission and I feel terrible about it."

"Well, these things take time."

"But I know why I'm not so far along." He twirled and rubbed the back of his neck. "Miss Hayworth, I think I'm having trouble because of a heavy conscience."

Heat colored the back of my throat. My body tensed. I must have had it coming. "What did you do?"

He looked at me. "I lied about my age to you because I wanted to be taken seriously, and that was wrong."

I stood frowning, listening. Waiting.

He looked at his boots. "I'm sorry I lied. That's all."

"That's it?"

He nodded. "I didn't think I'd see you again. I thought it wouldn't matter. Now that I've spent some time here, I don't feel right about it."

I shrugged. "Well, all right. Feel better?"

"I suppose."

Despite myself, I was smiling a little. "You're not the only one guilty of lying about his age. We all want to be a little younger than we are."

"Or older." He gave me a sideways glance.

"Oh."

There was a pause in conversation during which he cracked open a bucket of primer and dipped in a wedge of plywood. I watched him scrape it over the canvas.

"So," I added after a while, "Incidentally, how old are you?"

Antony let out an anxious sound like the puff of a couch when you land on it after a long morning. "Nineteen."

"Oh…my. Oh, my."

He abandoned the plywood. "I'm sorry, Miss Hayworth, I'll get out of your hair."

"No, no, why would you?" I backed away from him, the sight of his face and the wrinkles I now realized were dimples. "You're making good progress I'll come by and check later. Thank you!" I fled the house and ran up the hill.

Nineteen. I could hardly believe that every sound of every word I'd heard from him was only nineteen. Every line, every color, every impression by acrylic: only nineteen. I stopped outside my door and leaned over, feeling sick, but nothing came. I didn't want to see Antony again.

PAINT

That is, I really did, but I knew I shouldn't. Not until I could resolve my attraction to him, but it had to be done alone. Without counsel.

My goal was complicated by a network of dreams by night. They started as reiterations of meetings with my lawyer, except that Antony was in the room with us. First just watching, somehow unnoticed. Then he'd blow raspberries and tell jokes in my ear until it was all I could do to hold back laughter about legal advice. These dreams started out silly enough for me to believe they were merely a confusion of anxieties.

Before long, however, Antony's presence in my dreams was as singular and sensuous as a drop of honey on linen. He was never naked but somehow was even more vulnerable in looseness: his clothes were too tight or too large or too wet. Streams of paint snaked over his body and pooled in clavicular hollows. Heat poured forth from the base of his neck and when he looked up, the line of his jaw became the head of a glowing eel.

And there was that smell— it spilled over into my waking moments, a heavy scent: leather-like, masculine, narcotic. I opened my mornings with enormous breaths.

My determination to stay away from the boy grew with the frequency of the dreams. I was, and am, frustrated by an unsolved question: how was it that I became attracted to a *young man*, even one so talented? A type of person that I've rightly understood to be arrogant, unreliable and fickle by nature? I almost didn't give Andreas a chance, and he was a decade my senior.

Of course, a part of me wondered whether Antony's youth was the focal point of his allure, and therein I found rustling deposits of shame. I was disgusted by the infantile, girlish nature of my attraction. My reaction to Antony's age should have been no more than a source of mild embarrassment, but my pride was so strong I found myself harboring episodes of nausea and arousal by turns.

The flux tortured me. I wish I could restrict my thoughts to something else. I wished I was a man.

PAINT

It was around this time that I met Antony's uncle.

28

II

NAPPING LAMB

I found an unannounced visitor in my library, and he wasn't my lawyer. I frowned at him. My heart was in my throat, but I tried to sound angry. "Can I help you?"

He paused in the midst of rifling through one of my favorite novels and turned to face me. "It's nice to meet you."

I didn't take the hand he offered. "Let me rephrase that. Did someone let you in?"

In my mind's eye, a thousand images flashed. Women next to broken glass, bleeding from the mouth, dead in domestic spaces by the hands of men.

"Oh, yes," he gestured vaguely behind him. "Your husband, Pike." The man rested a hand on his belly. It wasn't overtly round, but it wasn't flat, either. "He's a fine chap."

"He is my driver."

The man seemed unfazed. "And you are…?"

I took a deep breath. "I am the owner of this house. I'm Eva Hayworth, obviously. Who are you?"

The man chuckled. "I'm sorry. I'm John. John Harrow. Mind if I have a seat?"

"Not terribly."

John settled himself into one of my armchairs and groaned. He wore dress shoes and a tweed jacket.

"Now," I spoke before he could open his mouth, "perhaps we could get to the business of why you're here? I don't get visitors often. Certainly not strangers."

"Of course." John folded his hands in his lap. "I was looking for my nephew and happened to hear through the grapevine—,"

I narrowed my eyes. "The grapevine."

"Yes, I happened to hear that he was under your employment. My nephew Antony?"

I touched my forehead and dropped my voice in the hope of sounding clinical. "He's doing a commission for me. A painting for my drawing room."

John laughed open-mouthed. "He's still painting?"

"I suppose so." I sat across from him and waited for the laughing to stop. "I like his work."

"You do?" John was smiling in a way I didn't like.

I picked dust off my skirt. "Yes. Anyway, I like to give opportunities when I can. A young man ought to have the chance to make a name for himself."

"You don't have any idea, do you?"

"Excuse me?"

"Madame Hayworth," John cleared his throat. "Antony is in possession of a large fortune. My sister left him a tremendous inheritance just over two years ago. He doesn't need to make a name for himself."

Seemed to me it was hardly fair for Harrow to make such a judgement.

"I appreciate your talking to me before roaming my estate for your nephew. Since you already have a relationship with Mr. Pike, I'm sure he'll give you a lift to Antony's studio." I stood and the man followed suit.

"I do hope my nephew is not taking advantage of you," John said.

I let out a peal of false laughter. I looked at him until he looked away. He said something, tipped his hat and left. I seized my novel, brushed it off and returned it to its spot on the shelf.

Later that same day, I got a call from Antony. When I saw the phone in Butler's hand I suppressed a deep sigh. I refused to concede that I might need physical preparation to speak with the boy.

"Hi, Antony, how are you?"

"All right."

"You're not screaming this time." I let out a chuckle and it was met with silence. "Are you— where are you calling from?"

"I'm in the studio."

"I see." Another silence. "I forgot there was a phone in there. Your uncle came by today."

"Yes, I know. I'm calling about that, actually." More waiting. "I'm not very well connected, Miss Hayworth, and I find myself forced to ask a favor of you."

I held the phone closer, pressed my palms on it. "What kind of favor?"

"I want you to direct me to some legal counsel. And maybe give me some advice yourself, if you are so inclined."

"Is something amiss?"

"The commission's fine, it's not that. I'm having an unrelated financial issue. If it's too much to ask, don't worry about it."

"No," I said. "Legal counsel is easy. I have a good lawyer you could borrow. Unless you think I can be of some help?"

"It's hard to explain it over the phone. Perhaps you could stop by? I can show you progress on the commission. Tomorrow morning?"

I nodded. "Tomorrow, ten o'clock."

After the phone call I stood staring like an idiot at the trim of a window, wondering what to wear and what I would say. Catching myself in this line of thought, I suddenly tensed and backed away from the phone.

I uttered the word "nineteen" and I shook my head at myself. But the next morning, I went to the studio as promised.

It was a dewy morning. He had strips of canvas tied around his hands.

"Did you cut yourself?"

"No," Antony said. "My hands just hurt some of the time." He took a stool in front of the canvas and I say nearby, looking at it.

"I hope you wear a mask, Antony. There are a lot of fumes.

"I have to go without it. It's the only way I can tell blue and black apart."

"What do you mean?"

"Well, they…they smell different. Blue is a little sweeter. I'm a bit colorblind," he added quickly.

"If you can't see the difference then why should it matter to you?"

"It matters to *you*, Miss Hayworth, it has to. Your jewelry is sorted by color." He twisted the canvas around his left hand, looking worried.

"You noticed that?"

Antony just shrugged. "Can I offer you something to eat?"

"Sure, why not?" I took a seat, and a few minutes later a cozy smell wafted out of the kitchen. Antony appeared in its wake with a round tray, which he set on a crate between us. He picked up a knife. I watched him butter some toast and then pause to flex his wrist.

"Let me take that, Antony."

"It's all right."

"Please. You're scraping it horribly."

He dropped the knife and tucked his hands under his arms as he sat. I applied butter with circular swipes. "Do you need to see a doctor?"

"I've seen a doctor already. It was no good."

"Is there no remedy?"

Antony sighed. "He recommended something, but I dare say it's a little out of reach."

I set down the knife. "What did he recommend?"

I was on the verge of biting toast; the butter was melting in a pool of yellow with black specks.

Antony's eyes were shut. A vein pulsed visibly in his neck.

I put down my toast. "Well?"

"I appreciate your being here, Miss Hayworth, but I really don't want to tell you about my health."

Like fire a fear rose to my mouth. "Why not? Are you very sick?" The image of my pale, dead Andreas flashed before my eyes for the first time in weeks. "Please don't tell me you're dying."

The saucer in my hand was trembling. Antony took it from me. "I'm sorry, I'm being insensitive. You lost your spouse, for God's sake."

I regained my breath. "That was embarrassing." I gave him an uneasy smile, which he returned in kind.

"I'm not dying, Miss Hayworth. I promise. Not any more than you are."

"Of course not." I sighed. "You wanted advice on something?"

"Yes." He looked at his knees. I remember this image.

I realized how rare it was to see a man regard himself instead of looking at me or out at the world. "My uncle came to see me yesterday morning—,"

"Morning?" I interrupted. I hadn't met John Harrow until afternoon. He'd not only gotten into my property without my consent, he'd gone right into my spare house! "Was he really here in the morning? In the house?"

Antony nodded. "I demanded to know how he found me, and he said that…well, he told me he'd been in touch with you and you were able to help him out."

"That's a lie." I shook my head. "I'm sorry, I just…that's untrue. Go on."

"I don't trust him either, Miss Hayworth. My mom…" He hesitated, then rubbed his mouth with the back of his hand. "He never got along with her. I know I told you I had work before, and that's true. I like to work. But I started painting when Mother left me an inheritance."

He looked up at me with imploring eyes. "It's not a lot, Miss Hayworth, I didn't want to mislead you. I just like to stay private."

I chuckled mirthlessly. "I can see why. Let me guess, your uncle wants a chunk of this money, does he?"

The young man hesitated.

"He knows it's my money, and I can prove it. But he wants me to invest in a business with him. I've told him I won't do it. I've told him several times." Antony's voice dropped an octave. "Uncle John never hears the word 'no.' And I'm wondering whether I should let him have his way."

"Do you want to take legal action?"

Antony shrugged. "I don't know. I worry about what recourse he might take to convince me again. I nearly fought him, the last time, and I don't want to make a scene." He adjusted his posture as he said this and I sensed that he was trying to impress me with they last comment. But it was a false impression, surely, manufactured by my lust.

"I have a great lawyer, Antony, if you want to work it out."

He cocked his head like a young animal. "I feel okay about it, actually. Now that I've run it past you. I'm just going to ignore him."

I took a bite of toast and chewed, thinking about how I could tighten the security of my estate. "He can't make you do anything you don't want to do." I looked at the canvas. "Can I ask you something?"

Antony nodded, swallowing toast.

I licked my lips. "Why is there a hole in the painting?"

Antony grinned. "To show some of the wallpaper through."

"Why in the world, though?"

"You'll see, Miss Hayworth. It'll all make sense in the end. And anyway—," he placed a hand on the edge of the canvas. "—it was a little too tight." He looked at me. "I like using stiff brushes, so the canvas has to have some buoyancy, you know."

"Yes, I know," I said quickly, feeling myself sweat a little. "I understand."

"I've got brand new ones," Antony pulled a bundle out from under his chair and unrolled it on his lap. "Don't worry, Miss Hayworth, I know you gave me a check but I paid for these myself."

"Antony—,"

"Now, look." He held one up between us. "This is a fan brush. See the shape, Miss

Hayworth?" He leaned obscenely close. "The bristles don't touch each other."

His bandaged fingers were inches away from my hand and I suddenly remembered the time when Andy had cut himself on a letter opener. "You're right. They're not touching at all."

Flushed and smiling, Antony returned the thing to its bundle. I put my plate on the tray between us. "I think I should go, Antony. Are you sure you don't want my lawyer?"

"No, thank you. I appreciate your help."

I nodded at him. "Antony, I hope you know that whatever your doctor recommended is attainable."

He froze. "It's not."

"Trust me, I'm older than you. You have to prioritize your health."

He was shaking his head. "It's not a question of finances, Miss Hayworth."

"What is it, then?" I rubbed my forehead. "Never mind, never mind what it is. Just promise me you'll take his advice if necessary?"

For some reason, the painter would not look at me. He was stroking the edge of the canvas. "Antony? Promise?"

His hand landed on his lap. He finally looked at me. "I promise I will, Miss Hayworth, should it become…relevant."

I asked him for his doctor's number, and I left. I don't like to ruminate on mortality, but it would soon be a year that I'd been without my husband, and some memories were proving impossible to repress. I tried to outrun panic first mentally and then physically, bounding up the hill to my house.

In the early days of our courtship, I used to walk with Andreas down a path that I now crossed with my eyes averted; a path that led to his koi pond. There was just a single fish in there, and he prized it so! Devastated him when it died. He almost cried. Almost.

Those early walks were mostly fun, although my chaperone, who I sensed was at least attracted to Andreas as I, had gotten steadily closer with each excursion until Andreas finally told her to take a breath and let us be. That was something he and I always had in common: we despised scrutiny.

Andreas. I turned his name over in my mouth, trying to remember when I'd last said it aloud. It was too similar to Antony, too similar a character of tall sloping *A*, too similar in the romantic curvature that comes with triple-syllabic names.

At home, I was greeted with the delivery of an orchid that, with a note from my dear friend Esther. It was timely enough to ease my sorrow but it did induce a healthy dose of shame. Here she was sending me flowers in anticipation of Andy's death anniversary and I hadn't seriously spoken with her since days after its occurrence. I was stuck in my grief.

I gave Esther a phone call, telling her about my new painting (though nothing of its maker), then put on my riding clothes and set her card on my dresser next to Andy's last bottle of cologne.

Octave was always a pleasure horse. I'm not terribly competitive, though I sometimes wished I rode with the regularity of a competitor. On this particular afternoon, I remember my mare being especially stiff and shivery.

"Settle down, Octave," I told her, "it's only a short walk." The earth was wet. After cuing her away from Antony's studio I realized she was only veering towards it because I kept glancing at the place. I blinked hard and rode forward. "Come on, girl, stay on the trail. It's just me and you again. No Andreas." My throat closed. I cleared it.

Octave regained the suppleness that characterized my first rides with her. I started to ride regularly again. My thoughts in those days were ever a cycle of repeated notes, Antony moving in and out like an A major chord, while a dirge took the harmony. Then, while looking for a book, I passed through my drawing room and froze, adopting the tenseness that Octave gets when she's heard a rustle in the trees.

A shirt was on the fainting chair. Like a napping lamb. Scented and paint stained and in need of laundering. I lifted it. Closer to my breathing, it induced the narcotic vertigo of my dreams. Antony's shirt.

Days later, I summoned him for an afternoon tea. He arrived smiling, but with a tired pinch in his eyes. I had just refreshed myself after my excursions to the kitchen and was setting down a platter of fresh produce when Butler brought him into the gold and navy dining room.

"These are seasonal," I blurted, gesturing at my platter.

Antony pushed a sleeve back and picked out a slice of purple carrot, holding it against the light. "They're lovely, Miss Hayworth. Like little mandalas."

"I thought so, too." I opened a small drawer under my china cabinet and pulled out his shirt. I turned around to find the slip of carrot between Antony's teeth. His gaze flitted between the shirt and my face.

I frowned. "Now, why do you look like that?"

Antony chewed and swallowed the carrot. "You found my shirt."

"Yes, I found your shirt. I laundered it for you."

He snatched it out of my hands, blushing. "I'm sorry."

"It's no trouble." I busied myself with tongs, putting slices of melon in front of him. I felt him watching me.

"Miss Hayworth?" He sounded angry.

"What is it?"

"I have to ask you something uncomfortable, but I'd rather you be honest about it."

I suppressed the urge to roll my eyes. Always drama with this man. "What?"

Antony lifted a fork, then put it down. He rubbed a hand on his leg. "Have you been…have you visited the studio unannounced? At night?"

My brow furrowed. "No."

"Of course not." Antony twisted his shirt in his hands and glared around the room. His eyes looked darker than normal

I sat down, pouring tea for myself and wondering what to say. What could I make of a question like that? I should have been thinking more critically, but instead I was eager to see whether Antony would eat melon with a fork and was disproportionately relieved when he did not. Andy used to eat fruit with utensils, and I hated it. *Use your hands!* I wanted to scream at him. *It's only fruit, what are you afraid of?*

The painter caught me staring. He scraped a rind with his teeth and I looked away.

"Have more," I said.

He shook his head. "I must eat the rind. Doctor's orders."

"How is that?"

Antony shrugged. "He says its an aphrodisiac."

I dropped the sugar spoon. "Heavens, Antony!"

"I got black chocolate, too. It's coming all the way from—"

"Stop it, Antony!" I took a frustrated bite of cake and spoke through it. "Stop, okay?"

"Stop what?"

I swallowed. "Stop all this leaning in!" I blinked at him. In truth, I wanted him to lean in. I wanted him to lean in very much. "I can't discuss aphrodisiacs at my table with you."

"Why not?"

We stared at each other. "Brazen," I said simply, and he turned red. "That's what you are, brazen. Asking me if I've made nightly visits, you fool. Of course I haven't."

"Someone has," Antony said, staring at his plate.

"Who?"

"Did you make this bread?"

"I did. Don't change the subject."

Antony looked at my oversized window. Then his fork slipped out of his hand, onto the carpet. I stood up and he gestured for me to sit back down. "Miss Hayworth," he said, leaning over to retrieve the fork. "I can't finish this commission you've given me."

I put down my tea. "What do you mean?"

His frown deepened. "I don't care for it. I know it's irresponsible of me and I've wasted your time and money. I'm just going to leave. I've grown bored."

"And when did you have this stroke of insight?"

"This morning." Antony looked at me squarely, wiping his hands on a napkin. I could tell he was preparing to quit the room. "It's like you said, I'm young and…brazed, or whatever it was. I wasn't going to tell you so soon, since I'd gotten your trust, I thought I'd see if I could stretch my stay a little longer."

"You're a bad liar, Antony. And you know you haven't won my trust."

"Well, then, this should come as no surprise." He stood and whirled around.

"Antony," I said when his hand was on the doorknob, "your shirt is still here on the table."

He returned slowly, and knotted the garment in his hands. They were shaking. My trust in him, though not absolute, had anchored itself in the consistency of his love for painting. I didn't believe he'd grown bored. His confession made no sense. I sat back in my chair.

"What are you hiding from me?" He didn't answer. Never had I felt our age difference so acutely. "I know you're hiding something. And not something small and silly, like your age."

"I really do regret that."

"It's behind me. If you have to leave, I can respect that, but I want to know the real reason why."

He still wouldn't look at me. "I told you already."

"You're not stupid." I sharpened my tone and stood. "Do not lie to me, Antony, and don't expect me to let you go without a reason."

Antony was biting his lip. He crossed the room and drew the curtains. My mouth went dry.

"What are you doing?" I asked.

"I don't want us to be seen." The room darkened. He was young, but still taller than me. I closed my hand over the knife in my napkin. He stepped into a sliver of light in front of me and I lifted the weapon up to his collarbone.

"Don't you try anything, Antony no-name."

"Miss Hayworth, you don't understand." He was startled. I could feel his blood beating beneath my knuckles. It made me think of fresh cut beets. Of a horse's hot neck after a good run. "I'm a danger to you."

There's a slim distinction between fear and excitement. Both are characterized by a magnetic pull in the belly, a flicker of energy in the chest. I'm acquainted with both, but in that moment, I couldn't tell (and can't remember) which one I felt. "How are you a danger to me?"

Antony swallowed. It was lovely. "I've been sleeping with a rifle next to my bed." My arm relaxed. "My uncle has someone tracking me, I've been threatened all week."

"How? In what way?"

"Notes. Nightly visits. Someone digging around. I thought maybe you were suspicious of me, or just playing a joke, but last night someone came with a revolver and confronted me."

His hand closed over my knife-wielding wrist. "I'm putting you in anger by staying, Miss Hayworth. Uncle John is an evil, perverse person. I really don't want him around you. You have to let me go."

We were speaking in hushed voices, now. "What did they sound like, Antony? Did you see what they were wearing?"

"I couldn't. It was a man, the last time." I could detect a bit of yield in the register of Antony's voice; his blood was beating faster. He was terrified. My hand slackened and I wondered why he didn't remove it.

"Is that everything, Antony?"

"That's everything I know, that's it," he said, frantic. "I can't hide anything from you."

"Stop, Antony, you're losing your composure."

"You say my name a lot."

"I do not!"

"It's okay," he said, voice returning to normal. "I like it." His grip on my wrist softened.

I saw how easy it would be to slip the knife beyond the reach of his collar, and with a single swipe expose him in the half-light. I lowered the knife by degrees, going slow so as not to provoke my basest instinct.

"This has crossed over into sensitive territory, Antony. You're to go into town today and report all of your suspicions to the authorities."

The painter bowed his head. "I don't want to do that."

"Have you something to hide?"

"Not really."

"Then there's nothing to worry about." I watched him sit and put his face in his hands—,

my God they were lovely, even in the shadows.
"You have to report it."

"I didn't say I wouldn't. Just that I don't want
to."

I sat beside him. "We'll leave today."

"You're coming with me?"

"Of course I'm coming." After our last visit, I
had resolved that Antony's well-being was my
business. He'd done nothing to deserve my
abandonment now. "Tonight I want you to move
your things into my spare room. You're to sleep
here, and don't go to the studio alone. Butler or
myself will accompany you. Don't argue," I
added when he opened his mouth in protest.
"We'll leave you well enough alone to do your
work, but we'll be around. I'm not taking any
chances."

Antony rubbed his chin. "Is his name really
Butler?"

"Yes," I said, suppressing a chuckle, and
failing to hide a smile.

"You know," Antony said, leaning his face
sideways in an unbearably appeasing fashion,
"I'm not at all surprised by your generosity. I

never expect it, but it's here and I'm not shocked." He bit his lower lip. "I still think I should leave."

There's little I hate more in life than interruptions, and flashbacks are the sneakiest sort.

I knew I was still there with Antony, but a separate film came unbidden to my mind, much like this scene is coming to yours: Andreas pouring me a serving of broth, wordless, unwilling to address some error he made…I don't remember what it was. Only that it frightened me, and made me angry.

Our conflicts were always like that. I never knew what actions offended me until he ventured to commit them.

"Maybe after today," Antony went on, and then he sat back in his chair. "Miss Hayworth?"

It wasn't broth. It was a cream soup. Something with coconut. Smelled sweet. Made Andy cough.

"Are you okay? Are you thinking?"

I rubbed my neck. "I'm sorry."

Was this to be my life? Accosted by memories any time I begin to reconnect with another person?

"It's nothing." I rubbed between my eyes. "We ought to at least report it, and see where that gets us. Your leaving is not going to make either of us any safer. I don't fear much." I picked up a fork and speared a chunk of pineapple. "Anyway, you've got to finish that painting. I haven't looked forward to anything so much since my engagement."

Antony heaved an enormous sigh. "You're at least as wise as anyone I've ever met."

I raised my eyebrows, chewing like a cow while some juice trickled out of the corner of my mouth. I swallowed. "Goodness, Antony, don't flatter me. It's not good for my moral health." I stood up. "I'll meet you outside in under an hour."

"But the painting," he called after me before I left the dining room. "You're going to love it, Miss Hayworth! It's called *Many Gardens.*"

I smiled when I heard the happiness in his voice.

When we departed, Pike grumbled about going out so late in the afternoon. The police station, he argued, would likely be closed, the car needed an exam, et cetera. He wasted a good deal of energy trying to tempt us onto other errands. Antony and I mocked him silently in the back seat of the car; it was good fun, though it was soon brought to an end by the boy's motion sickness.

Pike urged us to hurry, noting aloud that the car was nearly out of fuel and it was a hot day. I assured him we wouldn't be long, and felt tension mounting as we approached the police station. We met with an investigator and Antony wrote a detailed report, pausing every few lines to flex his fingers.

"You write with both hands?" I commented.

"I've had to learn. But I'm not as good with the left, you can tell." Antony lifted a sheet and I could see the way his handwriting alternated, as though the story was being told by two minds. I appreciated that the investigator did not take this verbal exchange as an opportunity to make irrelevant conversation, but I have no way of knowing whether this indicated focus or an anti-social spirit.

I looked at him. "Should I be writing a report?"

The investigator shrugged. "Do you know anything other than what he told you?" he asked, nodding at Antony.

"Not particularly."

"Well, then," he sat back and gestured at me with open palms. "You don't have to write one."

He flashed a faux-smile at me. I didn't like his self-satisfaction. He acted as though he were absolving me of something.

"Am I allowed to write one?" I countered.

"Yes, you're allowed."

"Then get me one of those forms, please. That's what I'm here for, after all."

The man tried to exchange a look with Antony, as if he was supposed to relate to whatever frustration I had induced. Antony simply stared back.

"She wants some paper," he said.

The man heaved himself away from the table and I bit back a smile. "Thank you, Antony."

Antony nodded, staring at the wall. He rubbed a hand through his hair and kept writing. When my pen and paper arrived, I rolled up my sleeves.

"I'm going to tell all about your uncle," I said, grinning.

"Don't hold back," Antony answered through gritted teeth, and I lowered my head, resolving to keep my mouth shut. Their relationship was more volatile than I knew. When I wrote all I could think of, I stood up to excuse myself.

"I'll be just outside. Meet you in an hour or so."

Antony glanced at me. "Be careful."

"Of course." I smiled and left.

I slowly roamed the streets, a woman in public, senses open to real threats and minor threats and potential threats. Andreas found it unusual that I was like this. He didn't understand, but I suppose the streets were made for him. He looked good in public. Everyone always liked him, and it made my life easier.

My outings with Andreas were far less exhausting. It couldn't match my fantasies of being alone, but his presence lent me enough security to flit in and out of shops on a whim and even venture down the occasional alleyway.

I stared at fixed points. I pretended I knew where I was going.

It was terribly humid on this night, I remember that. I swatted a bug away from my ear and ducked into a hat shop. I was grateful to see that the owner was too busy assisting another evening customer to offer me help.

I studied the lining of a bright blue hat and then flicked it disdainfully back onto its hook when I heard a familiar voice. I turned to face it. It was Esther. Her hair was longer than I remembered.

"Eva, you're here! I haven't seen you in so long."

"It's been a long time," I agreed, picking up the hat again so I could pin the conversation to it. "They don't make these like they used to, you know, not the same sense of craft."

"I quite agree, the materials are different," Esher said, examining a red one. "This can't be wool. It's puckered too much. How have you been?"

"Well enough, you know. Thanks again for the orchids." I looked at her. "They're gorgeous. I seriously appreciate it. I know they can be a challenge to secure."

"Not for a friend." Esther smiled. "I've been meaning to write to you about this mystery novel I found. I think you'd love it. You can borrow mine."

I nodded, feeling more distracted by the moment. My friend's voice and smell and energy brought me back to the days of my marriage and beyond, when I still vibrated with hope for my ambitions.

I found myself staring at the trembling dark feathers on a hat while Esther continued.

"…My husband's in the cigar shop. You should join us for dinner."

"Oh." I tore my gaze away from the feathers. "Thank you, but I have to be getting home soon. I'm sorry if I seem a bit distracted. I think of Andreas often," I said, surprised at my own transparency.

She gave me an empathetic look. "Of course. We can all get together later."

"Soon," I said, nodding. The foundation of my friendship with Esther can only be credited to her forbearance and emotional acuity. Wanting to save the conversation from my rejection, I asked her advice on the hats. By the time the clerk wrapped my purchase, it had grown late.

"The days are so long now, I hardly notice the evening approach," Esther observed. "Are you going to get back alright?"

"Should be. My driver's close by."

"You still have a driver?"

"I do!"

We both laughed.

"And anyway," I continued, "I'm here with my charge, the one doing the painting for my drawing room."

Esther smiled. "I look forward to seeing that."

"God, me, too. I can't stand those walls."

"Who is he? The artist?"

"Young man I ran into," I said. "He's tragically talented, maybe you know him? His name is Antony. Can't believe I just found him in the street. I was at my bakery when I met him; the place I told you about that used to have the chocolate crowns."

"They stopped making those?"

"Yes, I'm devastated."

We stepped outside. Esther took off her gloves in the heat. "I had a young Antony do some landscaping for us last spring."

"Really?"

"Yes, a very sweet boy. He kind of blushes his way through conversation, yes ma'am, no sir, and the like. My niece was with us for a weekend and he taught her how to fish."

"Sounds like my Antony," I said. "How did the landscaping turn out?"

"Oh, it's so fine." I could see a glint in Esther's eye that indicated she was searching for words she didn't have. "He put this fountain in, but it doesn't look like a fountain. It's quiet. It just shudders a bit." She made a peculiar gesture with her hand. "I wasn't sure about it at first, but I'm so glad he talked us into it. I like it more every day." She touched my arm. "I hope you can come and see it soon."

We stopped outside the cigar shop and exchanged farewells. I headed back to where Pike was waiting. This newfound account of Antony lit me up a little. I could see him tutoring Esther's niece on a lakeside the image felt so distinctly real, so wholly pleasant, that I started to wonder whether my attraction to Antony was really as vapid as I feared.

A block away from the car, I spotted a scant woman with heavy make-up loitering under a lamp post. Seeing a man approach her, I scoffed and then froze. It was Antony.

I clutched my hat box tighter and walked with my head down, determined to leave the scene. The car, however, was in perfect view of it, and I half hoped that Antony was inside and I'd somehow failed to identify him correctly. I was wrong.

Pike dropped a newspaper on his lap. It sounded oddly muffled in the car.

"That boy's not done yet, is he?" I didn't answer. Pike's tone shifted. "What do you suppose he's doing, madame?"

"I don't know what you're talking about."

"But surely you must have passed him on the way here. I can see him in my rearview mirror."

I looked at the back of Pike's head. "It's none of our business."

My driver sighed and let out a self-satisfied sort of chuckle. "He certainly knows how to look after himself."

I'm not proud to say this, but I glanced desperately out the back window. Antony was handing her something. It looked like cash. It was definitely cash.

Pike went on. "Artists are such morally depraved creatures." He flicked his paper open. The smell of ink wafted into the back. "You mustn't be too hard on him, madame. His job is nearly done. He's just coping with the challenges of being a young man today."

"That's enough," I spat, wanting to smack Pike for this last comment. "We all have our challenges. And it's none of our business."

I wanted to put fire in my voice, but my disgust was too overwhelmed by disappointment to do so.

I stared down at my striped hat box for an indeterminable amount of time before I heard the door open. I could sense Antony beside me in every way but sight, and my pain deepened.

"You've done some shopping," he said, and I nodded, too distracted to read his tone. I fiddled with the satin ribbon on my box and watching buildings glide past my window. Inside, my hopes collapsed like a thousand buildings. I hadn't realized there were so many until I felt them shatter.

Once we left the thick of the city, Antony sighed deeply and I looked sideways at him. He was rubbing his brow with his hand. Perhaps he was bothered by a guilty conscience. I faced the window again. The night sky, at least, had not lost its beauty.

III

SHATTERED BOTTLES

I still remember that drive. As the last bit of sunlight was disappearing from the sky, the car began to slow prematurely. Pike pulled over to the side of the road and both Antony and I clutched the sides of our seats. The driver pre-empted my inquiry.

"I told you the car was in bad shape today," he said. "Give me a moment or two."

He left the car and Antony and I were alone. I kept turning over the question of why I felt so much disappointment. I didn't want the painter to mean so much to me, but perhaps therein lay the problem: I didn't want anyone to mean so much to me.

Pike lifted the hood, and I wondered what he expected to do for the engine in this near-darkness. When he finally returned to his seat and shut the door I heard a sharp intake of breath beside me, which I pointedly ignored. I felt less committed to keeping Antony guarded, but my word was my word. I'd already told Butler that the boy was in too poor of health to remain on his own, and I was in no mood for more explanations that night.

Perhaps, if his conscience bothered him enough, Antony would be unwilling to move in as planned without my reinforced approval. Not so. When I finally got home I heard shuffling from my bedroom, enough noise to ascertain that he was taking refuge in my house.

I rolled my eyes and tugged a brush through my hair. Then I sullenly tucked myself into bed, remembering a night similar to this, when I had calmly convinced myself that the painter would run me out of house and home. At least now I knew he wouldn't need to, what with all this money John Harrow was so eager to fetch.

I wondered a little whether I was judging Antony too harshly. It's not unusual for men to openly call on such people as the poor girl by the lamp post. It's common, actually. But I never cared for common. Antony, young as he was, was still an adult and old enough to know better.

These thoughts fled my mind and were replaced with visions of Andreas. I never meant for them to happen, but as I fell asleep in those days, I was often overcome with the sight of him smiling in a glittering field, eyes pinched shut, laughing with the purity of an infant.

Around midday, I woke and kicked off my blankets. I remember feeling dry and hot. Butler was going over a ledger in the library. He looked up when he saw me.

"Late start today, my lady?"

"Yes." I looked around at my books.

"I wasn't ready to accompany your charge this morning. He didn't want to wake you, and was very impatient to get to work. He assured me that he felt strong today, though, and I persuaded him to take a crate of ice, just in case."

"Good," I said tersely. Surely if Antony could "look after himself" in one way, he could in all others. To disguise my pained indifference I mumbled something cheery about the painting and took down an old book that I wanted to read again.

I enjoyed it, at least for awhile. I thought about food but didn't make any. It got hotter and I moved from the library to a room with a bigger fan, hiking up my dress as I did so. It was annoying, I reflected, to have to carry a body at the same time as a mind. I've never really adapted to it.

Then I heard a somewhat unfamiliar rumbling and looked out the window behind me. I stood up to it, squinting. Pike was standing outside and leaning over two cars, one of which was mine. The other I didn't recognize.

Butler had not mentioned any guests, and I was confident that if he was made aware of one, he would have told me so. I marched out of the room and then promptly marched back to leave my book on the table: I didn't want its binding to melt in the scorching heat.

"Pike!" I shouted, panting as I approached him outside. The sun itself seemed to drip into my eyes. "Pike, what are you doing?"

He smiled at me, wiping his hands on a rag. His t-shirt was tight and moist with sweat. Regrettably, I noted his well-developed and frankly conventional build. "I told you the car needed a good look."

"Well, take it to a shop, then," I responded, shading my face with a hand. "Whose car is this? Is someone here?"

"Just a friend. He's come to check it out."

"I made an explicit request about that, Pike. We have to be very careful about people coming around here. I don't expect you to act as a guard, but I told you to let me know about anyone visiting."

"You worry a lot, Madame Hayworth." He swung the rag over his shoulder, facing me squarely. Something told me he was trying to get me to take a good look at him in this heat. "I only want to get your car fixed. Transportation is freedom, after all."

I couldn't think of a response for Pike. There rarely was one. I turned on my heel and paused just outside of the main house, thinking almost endearingly of Antony's eagerness to work despite the heat and despite being alone. Conversing with Pike felt so insincere in comparison that it made what I witnessed the night before feel even more unbelievable.

I returned to the library, but I couldn't return to reading. I was distracted by the sense that I'd forgotten something. Pike gave me the impression that he was trying to redirect me somehow. From what, I didn't know, but I've long had inexplicable impressions of people, and to be honest, they were often correct.

I took an enormous breath, trying to refocus my thoughts on the book in front of me and I suddenly dropped it on my lap. I looked back out the window. Both cars were gone, but to my memory it became clear that one of them had the same angular character as John Harrow's car. I frowned. Perhaps, I thought, it would be wise to check on Antony after all.

I stood up and smoothed out my dress. It hardly seemed logical to let Harrow's trespass go unaddressed, even if that did mean checking on his nephew. That said, I felt reluctant to let anyone see me doing so, especially Antony himself.

After telling Butler I was going for a walk, I left through a side door and started up the hill towards the studio. Halfway through my trek I found myself wishing that I'd had more water that morning, if not breakfast. I was sweating so much that my fingers were almost too slippery to retrieve the key from the front of my dress. It felt unnaturally heavy as I rotated it in the back door of the studio. The door popped open a few inches and I held my breath as I peered into the kitchen beyond.

It was empty. I registered voices and used the opportunity to disguise the sound of my entrance. I shut the door behind me, dropping my mouth open to quiet my breathing. It was incredibly stuffy. Something slammed, and I jumped.

"Why have you shut my window?" It was Antony, sounding more irritated than I'd ever heard. Leaning toward the threshold of the kitchen, I realized that the canvas for *Many Gardens* was so enormous that it could actually conceal my foray into the workspace. I tiptoed forward.

"The bugs are coming in." It was the gruff but unmistakable voice of John Harrow. "No one can think straight with bees flying around."

"I take no issue with the company of bees." I detected a note of catty defiance in the boy's voice and heard the window slide back open. Air puffed softly over the hand hanging at my side. I drew it back and realized it had been exposed by the hole of the canvas. I bit my lower lip.

I retreated into shadow, crouching so that the opening in the canvas was at eye-level, giving me a view of the room beyond.

Antony pulled a shirt over himself. I saw it swallow the slim of his back, slick as a sea mammal. He picked a jacket up off a chair and tossed it at his uncle. "It's time for you to go."

John Harrow wore his ugliest smile. Antony straddled a chair and sat so close to the painting that I covered my mouth lest my breath shudder the frayed edge of the hole. The boy picked up one of his brushes and beat it loudly against the leg of a stool. Harrow got his hand around one of Antony's books and drew it close to his face. "What's the point of all this, anyway?"

"It's nothing you would understand, Uncle John."

"Waste of time." Harrow dropped the book. "You think I haven't got any creative instinct, don't you?"

"It's not creative instinct. It's just human instinct," Antony spat, and I was puzzling so deeply over this statement that I almost missed Harrow's next words.

"You can't keep this up, boy, there are no patrons anymore. Commissions don't exist."

"There's a commission right here."

"Commission for what, son? Hayworth is just a lonely widow in search of a pet, and she's got it."

"I am no one's pet."

I frowned. Harrow's accusation struck me like a mallet.

"For the last time," Harrow said. "You know I have no intention of stealing your money. If you don't invest with me—,"

"I won't. I won't! Are you getting the picture?"

"Then I demand an explanation. A real one. Not the same excuses you've been feeding me about your finances."

"Fine." Antony pulled a brush across his canvas. "I will never do business with you, Uncle John, because you are a vile person. I don't like you."

"I'm not vile. I'm trying to save you from yourself."

"What you do to women is vile."

I heard a sound like the deafening bark of a jackal and I peered sideways. Harrow was laughing with a hand on his stomach. Antony took a chisel to the lid of a paint can and popped it open. "So you see why we can't work together," he said.

"No," Harrow answered, "you're a fool, boy. Women will drag you through mud if you keep up an attitude like that."

"I think women are quite nice."

"No wonder the widow likes you. She's overcome with lust."

"Absolutely not. Miss Hayworth is a person of great dignity and she respects me, that's all. I don't know why that's so hard for you to understand."

I shrank with shame. I never found such innocence and intensity combined into a single person like I found in Antony.

Harrow sat back. "Even so, there's no room in the real world for your sentiments about women."

"They're human sentiments, and we're not in the real world," Antony said. I didn't know what he meant about the real world, and neither did Harrow, from the looks of it. I presumed they had some kind of running philosophical disagreement alongside the financial one.

"You can go, now," Antony continued. "It's my mother's money and she's spinning in her grave as it is. I'm not going to change my mind."

Harrow folded his hands over his stomach. "Your mother's money. Is that why you're here, trying not to spend a dime?"

Antony's neck visibly stiffened. "I'm spending what I want."

"And I suppose you feel grand about that, don't you, son? Spending that dirty money."

Antony didn't answer. I saw his jaw muscles clutching. Harrow's mocking tone went on.

"Who do you suppose that money really belongs to, Antony? Who expedited all your mother's little dealings?"

"You're wicked and I hate you." Antony looked over his shoulder. "She entrusted the money to me. It's my decision." He washed the brush and banged it on the chair again. I saw Harrow stand up and approach the boy from behind. I suddenly felt nervous on Antony's behalf.

" 'To my oldest son,' " Harrow said, and I sensed that he was quoting Antony's mother. " 'Who is good and heroic, I leave my small fortune in the hope that his deeds will promote my absolution.' Don't you think that's touching? Do you suppose Ira is as innocent as you believe?"

Antony's voice was dryer than gravel under the sun. "Speak for yourself."

Harrow's hand landed on the boy's shoulder and Antony rounded on him so fast that the chair fell over when he stood. His face was inches away from his uncle's.

"You," he hissed, "do not touch me"

Harrow laughed, infuriating me. "Relax. You're just like your mother."

Antony smashed the man's face with a fist, and I nearly leapt with cathartic satisfaction, though I hadn't concluded what all this business was about Antony's mother. Harrow touched his bloodied nose, then threw Antony to the floor and kicked him so hard that I felt in my own stomach. I ran into the room shouting, but I was ignored. They wrestled on the ground.

I spotted a bucket of aquamarine paint and tossed it over them. They stopped suddenly, then broke apart. Antony wiped paint out of his eyes and shook his hands, spraying blue-green specks everywhere. Harrow put on his jacket and marched out of the studio as though he hadn't just assaulted his own kin.

"Mister Harrow!" I shouted, stepping over Antony's leg and following the man out the door. "You can't be so audacious!"

He ambled down a side slope, not going directly for the main house, not really going anywhere. He was ignoring me completely so I sped up. "This is my property, don't walk away from me like that! I've called the authorities, do you hear me?"

His pace almost imperceptibly quickened.

"That's right," I went on, following him. "No one gets away with trespassing on my property—, I know you've been sneaking in, here!" I could see he was making for the drive where I had spoken to Pike earlier. Antony called me from behind but I ignored it. "Harrow, you gutless coward," I shouted, "look at me when I talk to you!"

Harrow spun around and charged at me, and then we heard gunshot. I sank to my knees with my arms around my head. Harrow was backing up. I followed his gaze to see Antony standing in the doorway of the studio with a smoking rifle in his arms. "Don't come back, Uncle John."

Harrow straightened his paint covered coat. I went to stand by Antony as we watched his uncle retreat.

"I don't like the look of this," I said, and then realized that Antony was frowning at me. I approached him. "Are you okay?"

"Care to explain yourself?"

"Explain what?"

Antony narrowed his glittering eyes. "Were you eavesdropping?"

My face grew hot. "I didn't—how could—he kicked you!" I crossed my arms over my stomach when it pulsed again with sympathetic pain. "I told you not to be alone until we were secure."

"Miss Hayworth. You spied on me. There's paint everywhere!" He went back inside to retrieve a washcloth smudged with warm colors. "And now you want to chastise me." He wiped paint off his face with the cloth. "I don't need to be chastised; I need a shower. Unless you insist on supervising that, too."

"I don't like your tone," I said. "Move off my grounds. I don't need you or your painting. God knows what debauchery inspired it."

Antony blushed. "Debauchery indeed!"

"Shame on you." I could hardly breathe for anger.

"Me?" He looked so genuinely surprised, it forced me to wonder on what other occasions he may have duped me. "How could you possibly shame me? You don't know anything about my mother—,"

"No!" I shook my head. "Not your mother, Antony, you! You! I saw you yesterday with that poor street walker. I can't tolerate—no, I *loathe* that behavior. I hate it!"

Antony looked confused for a moment, then his face fell. "That was my cousin," he said.

"Your cousin?"

"Yes." He frowned. "She's very hard to get ahold of."

He stared me down.

Guilt coiled through my insides like a parasitic worm. He was telling the truth. "Antony, I—"

"That's what you think of me, isn't it? You think I'm *common.*" He rubbed his mouth as if the word were made of mud.

I looked at the glossy pool of aqua on the floor. "I jumped to a false conclusion, that's all. Who hasn't done that?"

"It was a false conclusion about my character!"

I heard him washing brushes, gathering them, and it made me nervous.

He went on. "I am equally guilty of false conclusions, Miss Hayworth. I thought you had great discernment. It was a fine justification for your wariness. But no one with a drop of intuition would accuse me *buying women.*"

"Antony, it's not that uncommon—,"

"I'm not common!" he shouted, slamming a book down so hard that I jumped.

Sweat dripped into my eyes. "I'm sorry. Forgive me."

"Have you repeated it?" He swiped an arm across his forehead.

"What?"

"Did you tell anyone what you thought you saw?"

"I may be without a 'drop of intuition,' " I said, the words burning me more than the heat, "but I'm not a gossip!"

Antony muttered something under his breath, then held the door open, gesturing for me to leave. "I can finish the painting tomorrow. I'll leave after that. You can get someone else to mount it for you."

Stepping over the threshold like a mouse, I glanced at the unfinished painting and saw a whisper of lilac. I wanted to say something clever or sympathetic, even demure, but I was still in a bit of shell-shock from his anger. Male wrath has always managed to freeze me up. If you're hoping to learn why, don't hold your breath.

"I didn't mean to yell so much," Antony said as I started to leave. I turned around. He was staring at the key in his hand.

"You were right," I said, "I spied on you. And you're frustrated. Understandably. Your uncle is not the most pleasant person."

"He's evil." Antony looked at me. "What did you see?"

"Oh…not a lot. Not too much." *Not enough*, I thought. *Just the dimples in your back like the hard hollows of a bitten apple.*

"You heard about mother?"

I sighed. "None of my business." As I was turning back around, Antony stopped me with just the shadow of a touch.

"You scared me, going after my uncle like that," Antony said. "I didn't know what he was going to do. You should be afraid of him."

"I am afraid of him," I said honestly, "but he just…he kicked you, Antony, and I'm a clod about you!"

Antony looked up, failing to hide a grin.

"I'm a clod about a lot of things," I said, desperate to cover my tracks. "I'll have a real word with Pike, that's for sure. He must have let your uncle in. Checking on the car, indeed. I'm finished with him. Who needs a driver, anyway? He's always hinting at a raise, and he's overpaid already. Greedy little monster."

"Fire him if have to, I mean, if you have to, Mayworth." Antony took a breath. "I don't like him that much."

"Mayworth?"

He frowned. "I'm sorry, Miss Hayworth, it's just so hot. You should have some water before you go…before walking back all the way."

I retreated into the shade of the studio. "You're right. Too hot for living."

Relief settled on me in layers. I could hardly believe how happy it made me that Antony was only helping his cousin. He prepared a pitcher of water and endeavored to put a lemon in it. He was just bad enough at slicing the thing to convince me that it was only for my benefit. I was glad that Butler sent a crate of ice.

Antony jabbed at it with an ice pick once or twice, then suddenly stopped, staring at the frozen slabs within. I peered into it. Nothing was amiss. I looked at him.

"What is it?"

"There's a—my doctor's number is on the window."

I looked at the window and back at him. "Sit down, Antony, I'll look for it. "

Antony nodded. It wasn't by the window. I looked back at him and he seemed incoherent.

Then, in an unforgettable and absurdly self-assured gesture, Antony plunged the ice pick down the length of his thigh.

I screamed and seized it from him. He was bleeding, but it was a shallow wound. "What are you doing?!"

"Putting it away. For my pocket." Antony pressed a hand on the wound and lowered himself to the ground, breathing like a dog.

I seized his face. "You're not sweating."

"Oh, Mayworth, my head is murder."

I released him. "I think you're having a heat stroke!"

"Are you sure? Touch me again."

I launched the ice pick at the crate, lifted a chunk out and pressed it against the man's neck. "Hold this. Hold it, Antony!"

I called an ambulance and got to work unlacing Antony's shoes. Confused, he started to pull away and I jabbed the side of his knee. "Don't. These have to come off."

Minutes later we hobbled down the hill, his shirt filled with ice and on his head. My head steadied his back, which was warmer than a horse, and it served to stabilize our little walk.

Upon entering the house, I screamed for Butler. "Ice! I need ice in the foyer!"

Antony crouched and touched the floor.

A disembodied voice called back: "More ice, Madame Hay—"

"Yes, Butler!" I interrupted, "Antony is having a heat stroke!"

"Cold," Antony said, spreading his arms out on the hardwood floor.

I touched the side of my head, mentally filtering for a hidden reserve of medical knowledge. I ran down the hall. I caught a glimpse of Butler and pointed at him. "Take off his pants," I ordered, then robbed my bed of sheets and soaked them in the bath tub. They became heavy. I dragged them downstairs with one hand over my eyes. I felt someone take the load from me and then Butler said, "You can look, now, Madame."

I dropped my hand. Antony was on the fainting chair, wrapped in wet sheets, trembling. You may as well have lodged the ice pick between my ribs, so difficult it was to see him suffer. I huffed. "Why is he shaking like that? Is it good or bad?"

Butler gave me a useless shrug. I didn't expect him to know, but somehow I found myself irritated. "I told him not to be alone. I told him the heat is dangerous. Imbecile." I rounded on Butler. "Why do men think they're immune to everything? Why?"

He said nothing. It didn't surprise me. All I could think of in that moment was how silent men were, silent and useless.

"I called an ambulance already, thank you. Very. Much." My voice shook. I went upstairs.

When I got to my room, I slammed the door hard enough to cause a chain reaction that dogs me to this day.

After the door slam, I heard a thud that I ignored. I was fuming, looking out the window, and that's when I sensed Andreas.

I threw my hands over my face. His bottle of cologne had fallen off its shelf. The last vestige of my late husband was seeping into the rug.

My mind fed me moments between us that I couldn't recall by will. Andreas passing me a blue glass, unsticking two pages in a book, giving me a sightless gaze from his death on this very bed—

I shouted like an injured bird. The memories were maddening. I tried to open a window—Andreas did it so easily—but it was stuck. I threw a shoe at it, and it bounced off. I went out into the hall, pacing like an animal.

It wasn't my fault, I knew, that Andreas was dead. Not my fault. Was not my fault.

But it was me. It was me. I did it!

He asked for it, came the self-soothing inner voice that sometimes accompanied this spiral, *He needed it. He insisted. It was an accident. You're not a bad person, and neither was he.*

Lunacy, I thought. Why, amongst all the healthy habits, traditional values and conventional turns of phrase, why did Andreas have to have that strange, dangerous, insatiable need?

I took a deep breath and stroked my forehead with a shaking thumb. "Men are strange. Ruled by their organs. I don't understand it. It was an accident. Men are strange. Ruled by their organs…." I heard a siren in the distance.

Antony was moved to an unused study room, one where the sunlight was especially golden at dusk. I watched a nurse put a needle in his arm. She threw leaves in a pouch of ice, cracked it against her leg and placed it on Antony's head. It started to slip, and I adjusted it. The nurse glared at me. I shook my head at her. "What?"

Antony smiled. "Jealous."

I shushed him and rolled my eyes at the nurse, but she made a little sound like "humph," and scanned me derisively. I gave her a series of fierce blinks.

"Excuse me, anyone can put ice on a man's head. If you want to be useful why don't you get a glass of saline?"

She crossed her arms, stood up and hesitated at the door.

"It's salt water," I added, "you are a nurse, aren't you?"

The doctor paid no heed to any of this.

I waited for him to finish polishing his spectacles before speaking again. "Could you check his hands before you leave? He has debilitating pain in his hands."

The doctor moved forward noiselessly, turning over Antony's arms. "He's a painter," I said. "It may be his nerves. I don't now. He's been seeing someone useless; they told him to eat aphrodisiacs."

The doctor gave a little nod. "Probably. You need to copulate," he said, looking into Antony's drained face. My jaw dropped.

Antony groaned. "Not this again."

"No, no, no," I said, my irritation battling my fear of appearing unreasonable. "With all due respect, doctor, coitus is not the solution to every conceivable medical problem."

"It is in the absence of a traceable cause."

"But—,"

"Madame Hayworth," the doctor said, squaring his shoulders at me. "I know you consider yourself to be very well read, but I have more experience than you. When these types of neurological issues appear in men at this age, it's often for the same reason."

"But that's not true. That's simply wrong. Incorrect. I'm not paying you to be wrong, I'm paying you to help him!"

"It's not your money."

"Excuse me?"

"You're very upset—"

"Don't patronize me. You're not here to diagnose me."

"—because your husband has passed." The man adjusted his spectacles and kept talking. My fury dissolved into exhaustion, which the idiot was surely counting on. No wonder his nurse was in a foul mood. I nodded my way through his explanation of Antony's treatment, ignoring the painter's mortification and transferring the cold pack to his neck.

I suddenly remembered Pike and sighed, scanning Antony's prone form. "Too bad you can't drive," I muttered, and then left to find my driver at the bottom of the stairs.

He gave me an asymmetric smile. "How's the young ward?"

"Alive," I said, sighing. "Come and sit with me, Pike."

He raised his eyebrows and followed me into the library. I braced myself. "I can't afford a driver anymore," I told him. "I'm going to give you a severance, but I think it would be a good idea for you to move on. To something else."

It was hard to meet his gaze. Pike did not blink; I couldn't read him. "I see."

"It's just, I would like you to leave. Please. It's nothing personal, I just. I want you to pack your things and go."

Pike smiled in the silence. "Must be really hard to live with your late husband's confidant, eh?"

"I…yes," I said, taking the bait, "that's exactly it, Pike. You see, it's nothing personal, it's more myself. I have to move on." I nodded with vigor placed my hands on my chest. "You know how us women can be."

In the back of my mind, my conviction about Pike's darkness grew. How could man be so cold, yet offer an emotionally incisive way out at the most unexpected time? And without blinking?

There was something else at play. I still felt like everything Pike said to me had an accusation hiding behind it.

He folded his hands together. "I can't leave now. I have to teach you to drive by yourself. At least that," he said, "and afterwards, you can expect the utmost discretion from me regarding Andy's death."

We stared at each other for nearly a minute. He didn't realize that I knew how to drive; at least a little. "He died of a heart attack," I said. Pike said nothing. I thought of the scent in my room and felt myself crumbling. "I'm not scared of rumors, Pike."

"If they are, in fact, rumors."

The nurse stomped into the library and handed me the glass of saline. "I don't know what you plan to do with this," she said, "but he doesn't need it. I gave him a salt lick."

"Salt *lick?*" I looked at Pike, hoping to take this opportunity to break some tension. "He's not a horse."

I took the glass, and Pike sat back in his chair. He watched the nurse leave, then looked at me.

"I'm teaching you to drive before I go. I won't leave you stranded with that animal here." He nodded in the direction of the stairs.

I narrowed my eyes. "Your efforts to dehumanize Antony are not lost on me."

He chuckled. "I know you're in need of an artist to rescue, madame, but your time would be better spent on someone more practical." He stood out of his chair and left.

I caught a whiff of petrol. "How do you know John Harrow?"

Pike hesitated in front of a window, his shadow covering the lower half of my shelf on pollinating insects. "Old friend."

"How did you meet him?"

"He's a business partner."

"How long?"

"Some months, now."

"Right." I gulped, remembering Harrow's pretense that he didn't know Pike was my driver. "I want you to go. Pack your things. Take a cab."

Another pause. "Why, Eva?"

"Because I don't like you. And don't call me Eva."

His shadow vanished. I brought the glass of saline upstairs and tried to persuade Antony to drink a little.

"It's awful, but you only need a sip. One or two." I helped him rise. The back of his head was wet from sweat and the ice pack dripping into his hair. I thought of checking his hands for nerve damage, but I couldn't bring myself to do that just yet. He turned slowly onto his left side, away from me.

"Easy does it, Mayworth," he muttered, and I frowned. He was likely delirious.

On the way back to my room I stopped on the stairs and sat, resting my head on my hands. I didn't want to return to Andy's lingering smell, but I didn't want it to fade without me. "I should visit Esther," I uttered aloud, but I didn't move. After all, it was too hot to go for a ride. Sometimes I wish I'd gone.

I don't know who would have read this far, or why. If you have, I would advise you to stop. You have no obligation to read more of these harrowing events in my life, and no need to know more of the darkness behind them. I, on the other hand, have committed to going as far as I can.

That night, Pike came to my bedroom with Andy's old pocket watch.

"I found this while packing," he told me, and stood still after I took it, as if he expected something. He said nothing of the smell, although I did catch his glance at the broken glass on the floor. I thanked him for the watch, but told him I didn't remember it.

"It broke," Pike said. "I was fond of it, so Andreas gave it to me and said if I could get it fixed, I could have it."

He was closing my hand over the thing. It wasn't ticking. It was deader than a body. "How about a driving lesson tomorrow, hmm? To refresh your memory."

I nodded, frowning. But the next morning, I couldn't find Pike, not even in his room. I'm ashamed to say that at that point, I still didn't realize that Butler was gone, either. He sometimes left for two or three days at a time to visit his sister, so I thought nothing of it.

"I fired Pike."

"Really? Fired him for good?" Antony froze in the act of spooning yogurt out of a teacup. It was his second day in bed, but I wouldn't let him leave until I was confident about his recovery. The gravity of the stroke seemed to wipe out his anger at me about eavesdropping the day before.

"I think he's the one who's been threatening you."

Antony set down the teacup. "I can't believe that never occurred to me."

"It may have been harsh, but he said he's done business with your uncle." I saw Antony's eyes harden. "And I just never…I never really liked him. I didn't know why; I just had a poor feeling. You know, last night he gave me this pocket watch." I showed it to Antony. "And he said it belonged to Andreas, but I don't remember it at all."

"Maybe he thought of it as a peace offering. A dishonest one, though."

"Maybe." I ran my thumb over the watch face. "He was supposed to give me a driving lesson this morning, or at least, he said he would. But he's gone. Probably for the best." Antony nestled back into his pillows and took a deep breath. Seeing him like that sent a painfully languid sensation down my midriff and legs. I looked away from him and tried to think of something less arousing, like shattered glass. Rotting food. "How are your hands?"

"No better. Doctors can be terribly obstinate."

"They're busy people."

"Even so. His nurse was a meanie. She stuck the needle hard." Antony looked at his elbow, where he was connected to an IV. "I shouldn't complain. This'll cost me a pretty penny, though."

"Antony, you really don't have to pay for this."

He gave me a hard stare. "Don't do that to me, Miss Hayworth. Please." He looked up at the IV bag. "I'm already bedridden."

Something about Antony's dignity made him seem strong and weak at the same time. It was early afternoon, I remember, but cloudy from the rain. My favorite kind of weather. "It's a shame it's so wet," I told him, "I was going to take Octave for a walk to the market."

I felt Antony smiling at me. Finally, I picked up one of his hands and turned it over. I pulled a stray feather out of his mattress. "Can you feel this?" I asked, rubbing it over the tips of his fingers.

"Barely. I think so."

"Don't look at it."

Antony shut his eyes and nodded. "I can feel it. But it still burns everywhere."

"Probably not nerve damage, then."

"Probably not."

I couldn't bring myself to release his hand. His bones were like a chart of tunnels. I curled my tongue in my mouth and scrambled internally for something to further justify my touch. "A woman in the market says she can tell futures from a palm. I don't believe her, though."

"Me neither." Antony didn't move. "That's an interesting scent you're wearing."

I released his hand. "It's, um, it's not mine. I slammed my door and it broke Andy's bottle."

My breath stopped in my throat. All at once, several tears fell all over my face. I pressed the heels of my palms into my eyes. "So sorry. I feel ridiculous. I can't believe I broke it."

"Oh, no."

I had the sense that Antony was regarding me as if I were the shattered bottle.

"Don't be sorry, Miss Hayworth. It was an accident."

Just like his death was an accident, I thought bitterly, and shook my head. I was nearly overcome by grief at this point and thought I should leave lest I be subjected to another man's indifference.

That's when Antony's hand swooped over to the side table like a bird to catch a bit of gauze. He dabbed the tears off my chin. There was so much pressure between his eyes; it was as if he was witnessing some kind of slaughter.

"He may have left his life but clearly he hasn't left your heart, Miss Hayworth."

I found this statement so hopelessly platonic and sensitive at once that I cried even harder. Antony swung his legs out of bed, seized both my hands and demanded that I look at him. The tears stopped at once. I was hardly breathing. Even Andreas rarely overwhelmed me with such undivided focus.

"Don't despair. Life is too fleeting for that."

"It is fleeting."

Antony sighed and shook his head. "Autumn envies you."

I blinked. "Who's Autumn?"

"The season autumn. The falling leaves. If you were a season, Miss Hayworth, don't you think you'd be autumn? I think so." He smiled a little and then released my hands, blushing harder than a rose in spring. "When I think about the seasons, it cheers me up considerably."

I'd never heard anything so romantic. I almost couldn't believe it. How quickly the heart can leap from distress to satisfaction with only the aid of a little excitement! As I write this, I think of sunlight breaking through a crack in an enormous cavern. That's how it felt. "I miss him, Antony."

"I know."

"He was nice to me. He wasn't subtle but he was nice to me. He liked exotic fish."

Antony listened. He was undistracted. "I know you must miss him dreadfully. That's why I cut a hole in *Many Gardens*. For the wallpaper. I wanted to put one of Andreas's flowers in that way."

I laughed. "I can't believe he thought they were orchids."

Anton smiled and kept listening.

I swallowed past a lump in my throat. "How is it that you have so much respect for someone you've never met?"

"It's not for him. It's for you. Not many people hire painters anymore, you know. You're rare."

"You have too much wisdom for your age."

He shook his head almost imperceptibly. "You have too much fear at yours, Miss Hayworth. You are full of talents, it's so clear to me. You don't need me, or Pike, or anyone else. I don't know how you can't see that."

"Antony, please don't flatter me if you don't mean it."

"I do mean it. You *know* that I mean it." He settled back into bed. "I thought I was fine yesterday until it was nearly too late. Just a headache." He seized my hand again and brushed his lips across my knuckles. "I owe you my life."

For the first time since I was a child, I had the devastating desire to earn the affection of another person. I had *wanted* Antony: his paintings, his company, his body. But in the moment that he said those words I wanted more than anything for him to like me.

It's a frightful sensation, wanting someone's approval. Worse than missing a step going downstairs in the dark.

"I don't want your life," I said miserably, in my most resigned voice. I shut my eyes, biting off the next words, which once uttered, could be as severe as a death sentence: *I just want you to be happy.*

"Anything else, then," Antony said across my unspoken confession. "If you need anything, please tell me. I'll do my best."

His offer transported me to the weeks after Andreas died. They were full of bouquets, condolences, tins of cookies and handshakes. If you ever need anything, they all said, tell me. I rubbed my forehead. Esther and her husband were the only ones who meant it. I cleared the table next to Antony's bed and told him that I would spend the afternoon at Esther's, and to try and summon Butler if he needed anything, although I still hadn't seen him.

I changed into one of my favorite dresses (this one a dark, satiny plum), and went to the garage.

I froze at the door, silent and terrified.

The tires were slashed, gaping open like empty purses.

IV

BLACK LEVIATHAN

I slowly backed out of the garage. I could hardly believe that Pike did this, that he kneeled with a box cutter for long minutes to ravage my car. His words seemed to echo in me: *Transportation is freedom, after all.*

When I got back to Antony's room my heart was thudding. I shut the door behind me. "He's here! He's planning something."

The painter sat up in bed. "You're a sight, Miss Hayworth!"

"Thanks, it's my favorite dress." I spoke quickly and hurried to the bed. "Listen, Pike slashed my tires and I can't find him. And I realized the cabs don't go out past six o'clock and he was at my room around seven." Antony's eyes flicked between mine. At least he was taking this in with as much seriousness as it warranted. "He's here, Antony, he's in the house, he's hiding, and I can't find Butler anywhere—,"

"Alright, take a breath, Mayworth." He put a steadying hand on my arm.

"I knew this would happen. I should have fired him a long time ago. I knew he wouldn't let it go, and now we're stranded, he stranded us!"

"No, we're not stranded. We'll be fine. We have a phone." Antony pinched the bridge of his nose. "I need to think. My rifle's still back in the studio. Do you think maybe he's there?"

I shook my head. "I don't know. Maybe he left by cab? But it's only ten in the morning."

"It's possible." Antony left the bed and walked over to a window, pulling the IV along with him. "Do you have any money in the house? Or something else he might want to steal?"

"Yes, in my safe. But it's hidden in the cellar. I don't think Pike even knows about it, although… oh, no. No." I put my face in my hands.

"What is it?"

I looked up, miserable. "The combination for the safe is Andy's birthday." I rubbed my hands over the silk on my waist in an attempt to self-soothe. "Lord, I'm a fool. We're in danger,

Antony. I've got a bad feeling, and I have hunches, you know."

I was starting to tear up again.

"Don't leave this room without me," Antony ordered, and his voice again by octave dropped, as I remembered it when he first accepted my commission. "Help me remove this."

He extended his arm and I put a hand on the IV drip. "I don't know, Antony."

"I'm better. I know myself. The nurse showed you how to take it out, right?"

I hesitated.

"Please," he added, and I found a piece of gauze.

Seconds later I dialed for Esther's house and handed the phone to Antony. "Tell her we're in danger and are coming to her house," I said. "I have to pack some things."

"But—,"

"I'll be fine, just going to my room. He's not in there, I always keep it locked."

I ran upstairs, pulling my key out from between my breasts as I did so. I rushed into my room, locked the door behind me and pulled a carpetbag from under the bed. Andy's scent was already changing from exposure to the air. My eyes watered.

I packed clothes, my journal and Andreas's daybook, which I never opened but could not risk losing. The rain had abated, and pleasantly round clouds were now drifting across the sky.

Just then I heard Antony shouting my name and running upstairs. He pounded on the door and I opened it. "Did Esther answer the phone?"

"No. Uncle John's car is outside."

I couldn't breathe. Panic flew through me like red leaves in a gust of wind. "Why? What does he want from me?"

"Do you have a weapon?"

I retrieved a knife from my bedside table and Antony reached for it, and then we heard a loud clank. I yelped. Antony seized my arm. "Was that a bird?" I asked, and we stared at the window with bated breath.

A second passed. The clouds kept drift by, and then in an instant, we saw the source of the noise. A flaming bottle rose up, made contact, and shattered the window.

"No—,"

It rolled over the spill in the rug and burst into flames.

Antony's arm struck the middle of my back with the force of an iron bar as he hurled me out of the room. We fled down the stairs and into the foyer, but we couldn't get the front door open; something was blocking it.

"Back door!" I shouted, seizing Antony's hand and running through the hall. We were coughing already, I couldn't believe how quickly the place filled with smoke. The back door was stuck, too. Antony hurled a paperweight at a window. It shattered, and we nearly wept with relief before realizing that the opening was just short of our reach.

"Cellar door," I uttered, pulling him to the ground and crawling.

Antony's hands were shaking viciously, and he still had a stubborn grip on the knife. We got into the cellar and Antony slammed the door behind us. We spent a full minute coughing, and then felt around in the dark. I made clicking noises to determine where the wall was; it helped a little. My fingers brushed a piece of tarp and I pulled it down. "I found the safe," I said, "The door is somewhere behind me, Antony."

"I got it, I got it." I heard shuffling, and then shaking. I recognized the sound of the latch.

"Push it up, Antony. Jiggle it." I ran my hands over the safe, trying to find the lock. It was an enormous box, taller than me. I found the knob but couldn't see the numbers. That was all fine. I'd rather leave with our lives than my money.

Just then I heard a splintering crash, and light flooded into the cellar, illuminating cobwebs and Antony's figure. He backed away from our escape route as if it were a cobra. He threw the tarp over me, flattened me against the safe, and the knob dug so hard into my side I cried out.

Antony started shouting. "She's trapped in the house, Uncle John! Go and get her, I'll give you all the money. I'll do what you said."

"I heard her. You're a liar. Edgar, they're both down here."

Edgar Pike. I thought of offering him everything in the safe; it was right behind me. I heard him lowering himself into the cellar, which at this point was getting smokier. It was all I could do not to cough underneath the tarp. And then, suddenly, clear as day, I heard Andreas's voice:

Be calm. There's a way out of this.

It was as if he was whispering in my ear. I had had no more vivid experience of Andreas since his death than I did in this denouement. I almost answered him aloud.

Someone seized Antony and pulled him away from me. The tarp fell. My heart rate slowed, I felt calmer than I expected. Harrow was pulling Antony into a most threatening embrace, with one hand holding a gun and the other in Antony's hair. A vapor mask rested around the villain's neck.

Antony thrusted the knife at him. It grazed Harrow's side and then Antony lost his grip.

"Don't hurt him," I said calmly. "You can have my money, Mr. Harrow. Don't argue, Antony." I shushed Antony with a finger. He lent me a desperate look, and his gaze moved to focus on something over my shoulder. I turned around.

Pike was pointing a revolver at me with steadied experience.

"Unlock it, then," Pike said. I obeyed and threw the door open.

"There." I hurled out a brick of cash. "That's what you want, isn't it?" I said, addressing Harrow.

I turned around to face Pike. He shook his head and beckoned me with a finger. I didn't move. Antony moaned horribly.

"Let us out first," I said.

We all flinched at a resounding thud from the kitchen above us, probably from the collapse of a smoldering beam.

Pike smiled. "Take a walk with me, Eva. I'm not going to let you die in this cellar. John has to have a little chat with the boy, and if everything goes well out there—," he gestured at the exit, "—we'll let the artist go, all right?"

He plans to kill you, Andy said.

Pike pulled a coil of garden rope out of his jacket and threw it over to Harrow, who was struggling with Antony. He fired a warning shot and I threw my hands over my ears, deaf with whistling for several seconds.

"Tell him to calm down," Harrow barked at me, and I did.

"You know he'll kill you if you don't listen, Antony," I said, trying with all my might to stay calm as Andreas suggested. "You know it's in him to do it. It'll be okay. I'll be back in minutes."

A vein stood out in Antony's neck. He was seething. "No."

"They have a deal, Antony, I'll handle it. Don't make a fuss. Please."

Harrow threw Antony against a step-ladder (I will never forget the sound) and picked up the rope.

Steady now, Andreas said, and I nearly wept. *Look at Pike, Eva. What is he wearing?*

Jacket. Shirt. Pants, belt. *Belt.*

"Good." It was still Andreas, but now I could see him. He leaned into the cellar from outside.

"Oh my God," I said aloud. He seemed so alive. There was more color in his face than when I last saw him. My mind, I knew, had a solution, and it was externalizing it in a form that I could not possibly ignore.

"You can do this, Eva," Andreas said, "don't put him off. Go slow. You know what to do."

"I can't…."

"Yes, you can," Pike said, misunderstanding me. He took my arm and led me out of the cellar. I gulped in the fresh air and he put his arm around me, still pointing the weapon with the other. "I love this dress on you."

I said nothing. I returned his hold slowly, reaching across his back and feeling for the belt. I heard a little hum of satisfaction and his grip on the gun slackened a little.

"We're going up to the guest house," he said, nodding at Antony's studio.

"Fine."

Pike proceeded to lecture me. "I told you not to get involved with an artist type. He has baggage, Eva. Vendettas. Harrow is a bit mad. I told him that the fire was a bad idea. But I knew you'd be safe, hmm? I was determined to see you out of there." He took the carpet bag. "What's in here?"

"Nothing special. I just wanted to save Andy's books from the fire."

Pike hurried me along. I practically had to jog to keep up. I kept staring out at the horizon, desperate for a miracle. I heard Octave screaming like a horn in the distance, announcing danger in the only way an equine can. Andreas walked beside me. He took my hand. The bottom of my dress was getting muddier, heavier from slogging down the hill.

Pike pushed me into the musty studio; the floor was wet from melted ice. He glanced regrettably at the bottom of his shoe, then took both off.

From adrenaline, I noticed the most peculiar details. A blade of grass clung to the hem of Pike's pants. I heard a gentle dripping near the ice crate. Pike went into the kitchen and I heard a clang that told me, somehow, that he had deposited the revolver in the kitchen sink. When he reemerged, his jacket was gone.

"Do it now, Eva." Andreas commanded. "A bear can't bite if you jump at his throat."

"Thank God you came," I said, seizing the front of Pike's shirt. "I thought we were going to die. I want you so much."

He grinned. "Of course you do," he said, and his hand was in my hair. I hadn't calculated this; if he took the pins out, if he had enough of a grip, it would be over. I made quick work of his buttons, but my hair was coming down. I saw Andreas over Pike's shoulder, standing in front of Antony's enormous painting.

"Focus on the dress," Andy said, "tell him you want help getting undressed."

Pike's face was like hot sandpaper on my neck, and wet. His hand was somewhere between satin and petticoat, not traveling or searching, but more immediate. I had less time than I thought. It was an onslaught. I'd forgotten that a man's touch is like an ocean, and when unwanted it has the pressure and aggression of molten rock. I was awake in a nightmare.

I reached behind me. "Help me get this off. I don't care about Antony," I lied, trying to sound convincing. "I don't want to rush. I want you to see me." I tasted bile after saying that, and swallowed it down.

One of many reasons why I didn't wear this dress often was its complexity. It had laces in the back, hooks in the front, and was onerous to put on by myself. But when Pike got to work on it, it took seconds. Like he's unlaced dresses of this kind a thousand times before. I never hated anyone as much as I hated him then.

He was saying something to me. Something about Andreas. I didn't care, I didn't listen, but it would come back to me later.

"His belt, Eva!" Ghost-Andy was distraught. "Get ahold of it!"

"I wanna try something with you," I cried, praying he would mistake my terror for lust.

Pike pulled the dress down. I felt exposed, but less encumbered. I started undoing his belt.

"Get over his arms," Andreas said.

I seized Pike's hand and pushed it onto my breast, ignoring the probing torrent of magma, feeling a thrill of hope when the belt hissed out of his pants. Pike was at my neck again, but my hands were behind him, arms over his shoulders, frantically seeking purchase at both ends of the belt. I had the buckle in my left hand. It was warm and slick.

"Try what?"

"Um, well…" I was trying to buy time. I slipped my right hand up, quickly brushing it along Pike's hair to get the sweat off my palm, and then I had the other end of the belt like the tongue of a dead animal. "I'm too shy to say."

I kept trying to slip it through the buckle, but I couldn't see.

Andreas was all but screaming. "Keep your arms up, Eva, pull from the front!"

I found the buckle.

Pike threw me on the wall with such force that I lost my breath. I looked at Ghost-Andy over his shoulder and sobbed.

Andy's neck was bruised and purple, darker than my satin dress abandoned on the floor.

"I can't do it," I sobbed.

"You will," both men said at once, real and imagined. I screamed. I didn't want to hear Andy. But he wouldn't stop.

"Listen to me, Eva!" His eyes were bullets. "Your anger is stronger than your fear, remember?"

"No."

"I yelled at you and you were so mad—,"

"I can't!" I shut my eyes.

Pike, heedless to this dialogue, heedless to everything except his own body, was telling me to relax. My inner mantra competed with the noise: *Men are strange. That's all there is to it. Ruled by their organs. I don't understand it. It was an accident.*

But it wasn't enough to drown out my husband.

"You were so mad at me, Eva, when you touched the crystal bowl it shattered everywhere." Andreas walked backwards.

Suddenly it was silent. I couldn't hear anything but the voice of this strangled ghost when he pointed to the satin on the floor. "You deserve better than this. He ruined your dress."

PAINT

I put the belt loop over Pike's head and pulled.

When he tried to peel my arms away I bit his arm and yanked the belt around to his front.

With all my limbs and nerves, by the skin of my teeth, I pulled. We were on the ground. He was choking. I pulled harder. He tried to get his fingers under the loop.

I'll never be able to say this right.

He kicked at me but I curled up, planted my feet on his chest and pulled the belt between my knees. Pike fought for his life as hard as I tried to end it. I couldn't look at him.

"I killed Andy!" I shouted, staring at the painting, the swirl in the corner named Play. The confession flew off my chest and into the man dying beneath my feet.

"I didn't mean to. He couldn't stop throttling himself and I was afraid."

"A little more, Eva," I heard in my ear, and I went on.

"He made me do it and I listened to him, Pike, I did what he told me to do." Then there was a crack and I felt a little give in my hands. Pike's neck was broken.

I dropped the belt, gasping. I gave the corpse a compulsive glance. Pike was bleeding from the mouth. I made a queasy sound and vomited on the paint covered floor.

Andreas crouched in front of me, collar open, smiling.

"Don't go yet," I whispered, "don't go yet." He pushed tears off my face with his thumb. I touched the bruises on his neck. "Oh, no," I wailed, "Oh no, no, *no*, I didn't mean it, Andy, it was an accident, with God as my witness I swear it was an accident."

He lowered my hand and buttoned his collar. "I know. It's okay. You knew I couldn't stop."

"Oh, baby."

"You didn't want to find me in a closet. Death by mishap."

I was breathless. "I'm sorry, I'm so sorry, every day I regret it, Andreas, my life is a nightmare."

"Settle down, Eva." He held my face, a gesture I missed more than I missed the sun in winter. The length of his fingers felt real, warm from the palm and cooler at the tips, like little spring leaves on my ears. "It was the right way for me to die. To ensure you never again obey someone if it doesn't feel right. Okay?"

"Okay." I wept, looking into his eyes, which betrayed their illusory nature in their stillness. "I love you, Andy."

The ghost knew he had little time left in a body. Too little even for words. In his final instant he pressed his lips to my forehead and vanished.

I was alone with a corpse and wearing only shoes.

I panted like a work dog. *Many Gardens* loomed over me. Split into botanical varieties by Antony's Play. Blue orchids in one section, misty lilac in another, a grove of trees and then the gaping hole through which I had spied the painter's back disappearing under a cotton shirt.

The dress was useless, I had no time to get it back on. I hid under Antony's brown coat. It was heavier than wet sheets. I wanted to stay in darkness but I pictured him trapped in the cellar so I stood up, grabbed the revolver out of the kitchen sink, and ran out the back door.

My house aflame sent a floating continent of black smoke into the sky. It was almost healing in its sublimity. I stared with my mouth open.

After this instant of hesitation I tied the coat —it barely reached my knees—and ran. I spotted Harrow climbing out of the cellar alone. I shot at him twice. The first made contact; the second was a miss. He doubled over and clutched his bleeding leg.

There's a kind of smile I really can't stand, much like the kind I encountered at the police station. I was looking at it right then, and I would have shot Harrow in the face if there were any bullets left, but I came up empty. I don't believe in killing. But there are certain rules of engagement that, once violated, cannot be reinstated for the party that did the violation.

Harrow kicked open the cellar door and nodded at it, as if to say, *go and get him.* Still pointing the revolver at him, I took as deep a breath as I could and dropped down into the smoke. My eyes burned. I saw nothing. Ash travelled up my legs, clinging to the sweat on the back of my knees. Then something bowled over me in the dark.

Antony tumbled out of the house like a blind animal, dragged the step-ladder tethered to his leg. I followed him, rolling back out onto the grass.

I heard his coughing, but it was a strange sound. His wrists were bound behind him. Antony was wearing a soot covered vapor mask. A little confusion visited my torpor. Why would Harrow let him have the mask?

I couldn't have found out if I wanted to; Harrow was gone. I crawled forward and pulled the mask of Antony's head. Like me, he vomited. It was black.

When Antony caught his breath it sounded like a desk being dragged across wood. He took enormous gasps while I fumbled with the rope. Soot thickened everything. I used the last vestiges of my strength to free him and then fell back, staring at the floating continent, huddled in the brown coat, coughing, coughing, coughing.

Eventually Antony crawled over to me, obstructing my view of the black leviathan. His eyes were eerily bright against the soot. "Miss Hayworth, please say something."

I tried, but I coughed again. He wheedled one arm underneath my shoulders and slowly lifted me.

"I'll kill him," Antony said, taking the revolver from me. "Where is he, Mayworth? I'll kill him."

"Gun's out. No bullets."

"I don't need it. I'll kill him, okay?"

My legs were gray and quivering.

"He's in the studio," I said, and I had the sensation that my neck was floating. Pain traveled in a line over the back of my skull. I grabbed the front of Antony's shirt. "I'm blacking out. Get help. Water."

He shushed me three times and gave me his shirt. Then I was back in the grass. I felt the earth beneath me shake with his footsteps. Poor Octave; she was still crying. There's no more apocalyptic sound than a horse in grief.

I tried to comfort her under my breath, and somehow had the notion that she could hear me.

PAINT

I wanted to stay awake long enough for Antony
to bring me water or news, but I couldn't.

V
FOUNTAIN

This is what I learned in the days that followed:

Antony rushed to the studio to find water and exact revenge against my assailant. After finding Pike's body, he searched for a spade in an attempt to bury the evidence, as he put it, "before the ambulance came." But then, realizing it was both impossible and foolish even with a spade, he stuffed my dress into my carpet bag, threw kerosene over Pike's body and burned the studio to cinders.

"I figured Pike would have matches on his person, and he did," Antony told me later. When I asked about the *Many Gardens,* he said: "I took a good look and that was it. I couldn't lug it out. Too weak. I really hurt my leg with that step-ladder, but I'm glad I thought to get your things. I thought we could make it look like he burned both houses and then no one would bother you about what really happened with Pike."

It wasn't until after the studio was ablaze that Antony realized he'd forgotten to call an ambulance, so shaken was he. But Esther, driving home from town with her husband, spotted the great leviathan from a distance. They drove up to find me in the grass and Antony nearby, holding my carpet bag. When he saw the car, he promptly collapsed.

Despite our daily walks, Antony's lungs were in significantly worse condition than mine during our recovery. This left me to deal with the detectives, one of whom was curious to know why I'd bothered with stockings and shoes but hadn't had the time to get on a dress. My lawyer was rightfully irritated by this line of questioning and held his ground, absolving me of any guilt in Edgar Pike's disappearance. The carpet bag wasn't covered in soot, but I told them I threw it out the window in the process of escaping the fire.

The rest of the story I fed them was mostly true: suspicious that my driver was collaborating with John Harrow, and after he made some inappropriate advances, I fired him. In a fit of revenge and jealousy about Antony, he ruined my car and burned down my estate. We gave them other details, told them about being locked in the house, escaping through the cellar, and about Butler's disappearance. I feared they would link him with the crime, and I was careful not to suggest anything to that effect. It wasn't long before the problem of Edgar Pike was out of my life…in my waking hours.

My nightmares about what happened in the studio are too vile to relate yet. Suffice it to say that for many nights I saw ghosts (among other things) and woke up screaming. When I couldn't get back to sleep, I slipped into Esther's living room to watch Antony battle slumber in his own way, making strange rumbling sounds as if he were trying to cough but could not. The doctors said there was a chance we could have fungus in our lungs. Oftentimes we both woke up and sat in silence together while Antony boiled a pot of tea for us to share.

I felt wretched for imposing on Esther and her husband. Despite all the years I've known her, we spent some of them barely acquainted because of my insular nature. I was secretly frustrated that I could think of no way to repay her for softening the vast transition that Antony and I were experiencing after the fire. We made efforts to keep her house but she insisted that we rest as much as possible. She even asked her trainer to help recondition Octave, who started spooking after the fire.

My vexation at myself translated to coldness. I couldn't help but see every interaction in those days as some kind of transaction, and it made me so uncomfortable I tried to avoid everybody.

The friendship, my mare, the carpetbag and a sooty stack of cash that survived in the innermost corner of my safe: This is what I had left, and I kept rotating this list in my mind as if it would synthesize into something more, but it didn't. I yearned for the moment when all I feared losing was the last of Andreas's cologne. The only thing

I have left of him now are memories, nightmares, and the daybook.

A fortnight after the fire I endeavored to put on the purple dress. There was still dry mud on the bottom but I didn't want to clean it lest I revisit the memory of how it got there. I just needed something to wear around the house. And I discovered that Pike had broken two of the front clasps.

I left them undone and marched into the kitchen. Esther's phone is next to her pantry. My insurance agent did not answer, as usual. I called the lawyer and couldn't keep anger out of my voice. He interrupted me to say that he was very sorry, but my last two checks had bounced and he could no longer afford to counsel me.

I stared into a bushel of apples. The regret in his voice was sincere. I apologized and told him that I would find a way to pay him, and then hung up before he could suggest a more charitable arrangement.

The tricky bit was that I hadn't reported the money in the safe. I hadn't thought to; it was the kind of thing Andreas was responsible for. I thought insurance was only for things: books, furniture, dresses. So aside from the ashy stack in the guest room (which I now owed to my ex-lawyer), I was truly broke.

I went outside, stared at the silent fountain and wailed.

Later, after persuading me not to take up the pipe, Esther tried talking me into going to town with her.

"You'll need a new coat for the fall."

My head ached. My eyes were puffy and still shedding the occasional tear. "I can't, Esther, I have nothing."

"That's not true," Esther took my hand. "You'll be okay, Eva."

"No. I don't know what I'm doing. I kept almost all Andy's money in the house and now it's burnt up. I'm too young to live out my days with whatever they'll give me. I'll have to find work. Like some—, some—, some common man or animal." I dropped my face in my hands. I hadn't told her about the checks bouncing. "Please leave me, Esther, you don't deserve the brunt of my nihilism right now. Just go."

"Wow, Eva. I don't even know what that word means. I don't know why you're worried. This is just temporary.s You're the most capable person I know."

"I don't want to be capable, Esther! I just want a man and a horse and a library, that's all! Lord God!" I looked up and shook the panic out of my hands. I remembered Andy's ghost and dissolved into a fresh peal of tears.

Antony was chopping carrots in the kitchen. He had a habit of slicing them into little mandalas like I made for our first tea together. I sensed some emotional significance behind this but I was in no mood to process it just then. We heard the strangely boyish and familiar thrum of his closed-mouth coughing.

Esther lowered her voice. "Antony's coming with us," she said. "He's looking for a place to live."

I could feel her gaze penetrating me. I tried not to betray any feelings about Antony, but

PAINT

Esther was no novice when it came to sensitive matters.

"Please cheer up, Eva. Please. It will do you good to go shopping, won't it, Antony?"

He joined us in the dining room with the carrots and some boiled beets. "That depends, Mrs. Bramley. You know Miss Hayworth very well, I'm sure, but it seems to me she quite likes to be alone." I nodded and Antony looked at me. The top clasps on my dress were still hanging open.

Before they left, Antony made me promise to take a vigorous walk as the doctor prescribed.

I walked the perimeter of the Bramley pasture and watched Octave graze on the dying scruff of late summer. She stayed within two steps of Esther's gray gelding. I sighed. The walk helped return me to myself. There were dustings of orange on the horizon, and even though I couldn't hear the leaves yet, I knew fall was approaching.

I huffed into my hands and tucked them under my arms. It was a good thing I had thought to take Antony's brown coat with me. He left for town without it for some unfathomable reason. And to think, just weeks ago the weather was bad enough for a heat stroke! I didn't seem possible. But then, neither did the fire. I watched the horses, wondering if they were sensitive enough to detect the apocalypse I felt.

I smiled, thinking of my first encounter with Antony. I had wondered whether he would run me out of house and home, and there I was. Not his fault, of course, but looking back, perhaps I got the story I was destined for.

As if on cue, I heard Esther's car pulling up the drive. It wasn't long before Antony joined me outside. I watched him approach, staring at the ground, wearing a crisp new black coat, his hair fluxing in the window like the outer rim of a lake. The wind gave his extremities a pink hue. It was misery to look at him then; he was a vision. I couldn't believe he compared me to fall when he was so clearly autumn made flesh. I straightened my posture, trying my best to disguise malaise.

"Those epaulets are very becoming," I said, glancing at Antony's shoulders.

He smiled and coughed. "I thought it was time I should get new clothes. How do you like my old coat?"

"Oh." I looked down at myself. "Well, it's very warm, and I promised I'd take a walk like you said."

Octave snorted and did a few little kicks. Antony said her name twice and she trotted up, little clouds of mist puffing out of her nostrils. He rubbed the blaze on her face. I watched, confused.

"Octave hates men," I said, and Antony suppressed another cough.

"Really?" he said, pulling a burr out of her forelock. "She's quite warm to me. I visited her a lot while painting *Many Gardens.*" He paused after that, holding the animal's face. "Wish I knew how to ride a horse."

What a sight that could be. He had the legs for it. Esther's gelding nickered and Octave bounded away from us to join her new companion.

"They're pair bonding," I said, then fell into a little coughing fit. Antony patted my back and his hand lingered after I caught my breath. "Horses are supposed to pair bond. I'm glad she can finally do it."

"Certainly. God makes things in pairs, after all."

I looked at Antony, my face suddenly tense. I didn't trust myself to speak. He looked so serious it almost didn't suit him. "I know it's cold," he said, "but could we walk just a little bit longer?"

I nodded. He took my hand and led me into a copse of trees, once of which was already orange and shedding. We sat on a small stone bench. I was suddenly nervous, and almost fell to talking before he could say anything that I wasn't prepared to hear, but my fatigue kept me quiet. I didn't want to talk. I didn't want to open my mouth to the cold air. But he had held my hand all this way and I knew that it couldn't be for nothing.

"I'm so sorry about your house, Miss Hayworth." His hands were on mine and gloved in leather, Lord God. "I fear I've been a part of this irreversible, huge disruption on your life, and I don't know how to repay you. Or the Bramleys, for that matter."

I nodded with my eyebrows raised, conceding to that point. I flexed my fingers. He took off his gloves and insisted that I put them on. It was like reaching into a warm basket of kittens. I sighed. "It's not your fault, Antony."

He had a couple of rumbling coughs and went on.

"Miss Hayworth, I feel that I've barely begun to know you. And I know that I…" He fixed his gaze on a branch above my head. "I'm significantly younger than your late husband, and I'm not in the best of health." He stood up and started pacing to and fro. He picked a leaf off a tree and stared at its veins. "I want to know you better."

I cleared my throat. "That's very nice, Antony. I want to know you better, too. Could we perhaps continues this discussion inside the house?"

He nodded and I started walking towards the pasture. I stopped and looked behind me. Antony hadn't moved. He was picking a rock out of the ground with the toe of his boot. As I watched him, my vision brightened by degrees while the sun reappeared from behind a cloud, giving us a bit of relief. "You don't want to go in yet?"

Antony looked up at the leaves, down at the rock, then back at me, his fists swiveling for warmth in his pockets.

"You could do anything," he said suddenly, in a tone I'd never heard from him.

"What are you talking about?"

"You can have any future, Mayworth."

"Thanks again, Antony, but I'm not a charity case. We'll both be just fine, all right?"

"No." He walked up to me. "You're not listening, please listen to me, Miss Hayworth. It took me a very long time to know what I'm going to say to you."

The wind pushed hair into my vision and Antony brushed it out of my face, tucking a lock behind my ear. He was taking shallow breaths in an effort not to cough.

"I don't want to insult you, that's all I mean by it. You could have any future you want. I believe that. And given what's transpired, I'm sure you don't crave the company of men. I just want to say." He stopped, biting his lip (Lord *God*). He took my hand and led me to the bench again. I tried in vain to keep bewilderment off my face.

Antony's voice changed again. "Miss Hayworth, I know I must be hopelessly unappealing to you, I just want to say that if you prefer the security of married life, and find yourself wanting to rebuild your home with a partner and a friend, I would marry you. And then you could…you know, you could have the money, and a new name if you want."

"Antony. I don't. I'm not." I babbled and shook my head.

He dropped my hand. "I know my background is questionable, but I'll share it if you want to know. And I'm pretty sure I can track down my birth certificate. It's just an offer, Miss Hayworth, you don't have to take it. It wouldn't have to mean anything. I just wanted to offer. A serious offer," he added.

"Antony, I do *not* find you unappealing, believe me. But I'm almost thirty. You're young and you can have any woman you like. I'm sure there are at least a couple girls in town with their eyes on you. Don't waste your fortune on me. I'm difficult."

"With all due respect, my mother told me to marry a proper lady or marry no one at all."

He did not cough. His spoke from the lowest part of his stomach, from a source of desire I'd never witnessed in another. The leaves above us made spots of light flutter on his cheekbones.

I took a shuddering sigh. "Antony, I'm not a proper lady. I come from money, I'm educated, but I'm not…people in town think I killed my husband. I tried to start a literacy program for years and I couldn't get any support. They talk about me. You deserve better."

"But you're innocent of what they say!"

"I still feel like a murderer."

"You're not. Pike was going to kill us."

Tears heated my eyes. I nearly told him the truth. *It was a complete accident, Antony, but I did it. I killed the man I loved and I don't think I can ever marry again.*

"Perhaps." I handed back his gloves and trudged back to the house.

I stayed in my room for the rest of the evening, but I wasn't depressed. Antony's kind words invigorated me. An inner confidence flickered to life; I trusted my ability not to succumb to despair. After all, I had resisted his proposal, which was far more tempting. I set myself to the unpleasant task of finally counting my ashy bills and starting a ledger. Esther joined me in my room with a lavender hat-box and a classics library under one arm. I sat up a little in my chair. "Did you get a new hat?"

Esther set it down on the bed. "You're feeling much better."

I nodded and pointed at the box. "Let me see what you got."

She pulled a pin out of her hair. "Actually, it's yours. And the books, too. Antony bought them. He just asked me to give them to you."

"Oh…." I turned back to the desk, feeling Esther's eyes on me.

"He was excited to help you restart your collection."

"I see."

"Eva?"

"Hmm?"

"Will you look at me?"

I turned around. Esther looked confused. I stared at the hat-box.

"He proposed," I said in a deadpan voice. "Marriage."

Esther leapt onto the bed. "Fantastic! What a relief. He has such affection for you."

"What do you mean?"

Esther blinked. "Isn't it obvious?"

I put my hair behind me. "I don't know, Esther. You're much better than I at picking up on these things. Anyway, I can't take these gifts. I told him no."

Esther's eyes widened a little. "You're joking."

"I'm not."

"But aren't you—don't you want him? Have you seen him, Eva?"

The question unseated me. "Well, Esther, I mean, yes, of course I want him, he's the picture of male beauty, but I also want cake for breakfast every morning. What I want is hardly the point."

"He would disagree with you on that."

I folded my ledger. "It was kind of him, but only a formality. He's too young. I have no right to accept. He was just trying to do the right thing."

Esther twisted her mouth a bit. "I dunno, Eva," she said in the sort of city-voice I'd never really acquired, "he's a free spirit. An artist. Doesn't strike me as a type who would do something like that just as a formality."

"That's not how he made it sound."

"But of course he can't make it like he's proposing out of passion, Eva, you're a proper lady!"

There it was again: proper lady. I leaned my head on my hand.

"I don't feel like that. I feel woefully inadequate." I imagined Antony giving a last look at his painting before burning Pike's body, just to save me from questions. "He's different than me. He does things I don't think I could have the bravery to do."

But just as I said this aloud, I realized it was a lie. It took courage to strangle Pike.

"You shouldn't marry him if you don't want to," Esther said. "And you don't *need* to. But for heaven's sake, don't tell me you can't see that his affection is sincere. Lord, you're not that dense. You can't be." She lifted the hat-box. "It took him forty-five minutes to pick this out. It drove me batty, Eva! He made them change the pin with another hat."

I laughed and bit my lower lip. "Okay, let me see it."

She passed it to me and I pulled the ribbon loose. I was surprised at how much peace it brought me to just lift the tissue paper, to feel that amongst all the disaster I could have a small moment with something new.

It was an asymmetrical indigo hat, with a glittering scarlet pin in the shape of a maple leaf. I put my hand on my forehead.

"Oh God, Esther, he told me I was autumn." I closed the box and gave it back to her. "I can't take this. I can't take the books either," I said, though I was eyeing them with a very particular lust.

That night, after an especially disturbing nightmare in which I was trapped in an elevator with a child-version of Pike, I woke up to something unusual. Silence.

On my way to the kitchen for midnight tea, I paused outside Antony's door. It was shut. My fist hesitated in midair. I didn't want to risk waking or upsetting him. After what happened, it was only fair that he should initiate our next interaction.

I started heating the kettle and glanced out the window above the sink. Antony was sitting out in the moonlight.

He stared at the fountain and wept. He coughed and spat. I would say that he looked defeated, but it wasn't defeat. Maybe he was just to young to give up. What I saw was distress.

I took a deep breath and stared at the kettle. After a while, I felt Antony soundlessly reenter the kitchen on my right. He lifted the kettle off just before it screamed so as not to wake up the Bramleys. I ordered him to sit.

"I've watched you make tea for us enough times, Antony. Let me do it."

He thanked me and sat. After I put down steaming tea cups and sat across from him, he finally spoke.

"Esther tried to return the books, but I'd rather you keep them."

"I can't—,"

"That's not a request, Eva," he said harshly, and then shook his head and said something apologetic.

I didn't hear it. His voice on my first name was echoing through the deepest regions of my body.

He went on. "Please keep the books, Miss Hayworth. I'd feel remiss if you didn't have something good to read."

I stirred my tea, then took Antony's hand on the table and squeezed it so hard I thought I saw him flinch.

"I thought so." Antony took a careful, slow breath. "My mother said that women are always in need of a great adventure."

In a single stroke, I understood the meaning of what had transpired since the day I met

Antony. I crossed my legs and brushed his feet under the table. Back when I took off his shoes in the studio to counteract the heat stroke, I noted his doe-like ankles, the toes descending with mathematical precision. I shut my eyes. Sitting there in the moonlight, listening to his half-coughs and recovering from our mutual nightmares, I felt flat and light. Like the endpaper of a novel.

I lifted Antony's hand to my lips.

Imagine these colors: A sheet of turquoise overcome by dripping black. Horizontal lines of deep purple. This is the sensation of having a painter's index finger in your mouth.

Antony hid his face in his forearm for a few seconds. He shifted in his chair and I released him. I said his name and he looked at me, eyes glinting like rare gems.

I sipped my tea. "Where's your birth certificate?"

Antony grinned. "In a brothel."

I smiled back at him over the rim of my teacup. Adventure, indeed.

Ayah is an indie novelist, filmmaker, speaker and content creator. It is her life's mission to share the fusion of narratology and metaphysics by means of fiction.

For updates, join the Making Metafiction newsletter at shethewriter.com

artist credits

// cover art //

illustration by Ana Dragičević

design from fiverr.com/marmarko78

//unsplash artists //

PAINT front page by Shraga Kopstein

part two facing page by Mutzii

part two facing page by Lurm

part three facing page by Greta Pichetti

part four facing page by Fredrick Kearney Jr.

part five facing page by Simon Matzinger

author biography facing page by Louis Maniquet